I0681101

STORIES OF
DISILLUSIONMENT

by

JAMES I. MCGOVERN

WingSpan Press

Published in the United States and the United Kingdom by WingSpan Press, Livermore, CA

The WingSpan name, logo and colophon are the trademarks of WingSpan Publishing.

ISBN 978-1-63683-050-6 (pbk.)
ISBN 978-1-63683-960-8 (ebk.)

First edition 2023

Printed in the United States of America

www.wingspanpress.com

"Something which I thought I was seeing with my eyes is in fact grasped solely by the faculty of judgment which is in my mind."

—Descartes, *Meditations on First Philosophy*

CONTENTS

Aegean Omens 1

Timeshare Rental 17

White Sands 31

The Secluded Literatus 41

The Demotions...49

Executioner 59

Qualities of Mercy 69

The Tower Home 77

A Superior Maid...89

Property Lines 103

The Lake Isle...117

Hummingbirds in Winter 129

AEGEAN OMENS

In my youth I taught for a while at a progressive school on a Greek island. My memories of then are dominated by conversations with Cybil, another teacher, on the island's rocky shore. She was a fellow American and taught meditation and tennis, having gone there with two girlfriends who taught math and science. I was the school's English instructor and handled the soccer team, assisted by a Frenchman who taught his own language and German. The only other teachers were a Briton teaching economics/history and an Italian lady doing music and art. Our headmaster was a mercurial Greek tycoon, the support staff also Greek except for the Japanese chef, the headmaster desiring variety in his diet. Our student body numbered fourteen, down from 23 the previous year. The school had experienced some growing pains.

In addition to our both being American, Cybil and I shared commonality in being the only two head coaches. Her tennis team consisted of four players, three female students and a lone male who also played soccer. The Frenchman and I had the entire male population on our team, but we were still two short of a starting lineup, so I had to request opposing coaches to also play two players short. They were usually sporting about it.

It was always evening when Cybil and I would find each other on the shore, at first accidentally then increasingly by design. By then the sun was low, the distant mainland fading, the sea reclaiming its prominence. We'd walk awhile or sit on a large flat rock.

1

"So why did you come here?" she asked early on.

"Well, teaching jobs were scarce back home so I tapped into positions abroad. Even then, it was either here or Dar-es-Salaam."

She smiled in the oblique dying rays. She had maple brown hair in a page boy style, ivory complexion, and a frequent squint as if concentrating or in need of glasses. She was average height and slim to slightly athletic in build.

"What about yourself?" I asked.

"I'd been in a meditative commune in Majorca with my then-boyfriend. When that ended I couldn't see returning to Michigan so, like you, I checked around and found this place. It was just starting then and needed teachers, so I pressed Makis to hire Jill and Heidi along with me. To my surprise he happily went along."

"I take it you three are quite close."

"Close, yes. Quite close is just Jill and Heidi."

"Oh. Okay."

"None of us were teachers in the States. Technically not qualified. Hope you don't mind working with amateurs."

"Hey, I feel like one myself. Anyway, you have a year of experience now, the last year here."

"I don't know if that'll count. It got pretty crazy. Makis can be kind of weird at times, unpredictable. The people sending their kids here are diplomats, bankers, corporate types. A bad rep spreads fast among the rich."

"Yes, I suppose so."

"Might be better this year, though. He seems to have mellowed a bit."

The first few weeks were, in fact, unremarkable. The classes and activities passed as they would at any residential school, though with a few odd details. Attendance at class was optional and no grades were given, brief progress reports supplied to parents each month. The students slept in a co-ed dorm, even though another and larger dorm stood unused. The faculty, on the other hand, was segregated by gender into cottages that had once been barracks. A sophisticated, newly-installed security system had cameras spying throughout the campus, indoors and out.

"The big man is hosting a party this Saturday," Lucien advised me at the soccer field. "Much wine will flow."

"Think so? I heard he's settled down after last year."

"Hm, yes. That is what he'd want people to think."

One of the boys on the field tripped over the ball while dribbling. My assistant stroked his beard thoughtfully.

"You know," he said, "none of these would make the team at most schools."

"It would be nice to win at least one."

"Perhaps a forfeit. Unfortunately, we are always the visitors due to the travel over water. The others have only to get to their home fields."

The party, as it turned out, was a major letdown. The only outside guests were five people who arrived by private yacht, rather than ferry, with the crew remaining aboard for a return trip. At least one crewman was armed. The guests consisted of two middle-aged couples and an elderly man, all formally dressed. They joined us faculty members in Great House, the headmaster's old, expansive residence. He introduced each of us along with our disciplines, but did not identify the visitors. The two female guests murmured comments of greeting, their apparent husbands giving nods, the elderly fellow inert. They soon left with Makis for a smoking lounge some distance from the party room. We were left with punch bowl and sushi trays, and with two maintenance men playing recorders. Violetta the music instructor honored us with a song. We all soon drifted away as the smoking lounge doors did not open.

The incident was mostly a joke when I met with Cybil later, but it fueled my curiosity about Makis.

"So who were those outsiders he invited?" I asked.

"The chairmen of two large businesses and a deposed royal. Makis wants to restore him to get a foothold in industry there. A bunch of others were invited but they're leery, sent regrets."

"Last year's bad publicity."

"Right."

"Yet you and your friends came back."

"It's still a good deal for us. We're able to work together here, a near paradise after Michigan, and for great pay. Most of the other teachers left."

"You all get along with Makis pretty well? His personality?"

Cybil looked thoughtful, gazed out at the timeless sunset, its orange and purple majesty, the darkening sea.

"Personality," she repeated. "More like his essence. He's incredibly independent, against all banal conventions. It's there in his physical self even--the height, the broadness, his heavy features and curly black hair oiled back. And his laugh, the way he can fend off anything you say. And yet he can seem so sensitive, compassionate."

I hesitated, then smiled.

"You're rather attached to him, it seems."

She looked directly at me.

"He's a true progressive, not like those who claim the word but just chant mantras for pretentious causes. He stands for quality, and for people who value it above all the nonsense of our ignorant world. If someone says he's elitist, he'll say 'So what? Long live the elite!'"

———

Our meetings became less frequent after the discussion of Makis, also shorter with our talk growing forced. But they had to continue, it seemed, for our witnessing of the dusk, as if it affirmed our belief in something greater than our day-to-day, however vague or unattainable it was. An obstacle stood in the way of our intimacy, a presence on the island behind us. The ubiquitous security cameras suggested a controlling power before which genuine love would shrivel. *You are being watched*, came the message, and spontaneity was gone.

As I sat in the faculty lounge one day perusing students' papers, I was approached by Cybil's friend Heidi, the science teacher. She was a slender young woman with blond braids and faded freckles. She described an outing she was having for her astronomy club, taking several students up the headland to view the stars and planets, identify constellations and such.

"There's the equipment to bring along," she said, "bulky but delicate. I'd rather not trust it to the students. Would you like to come with and assist me? Cybil said you like the night sky."

I could hardly refuse. We were a small community and needed to cooperate with each other for things to work. I wondered, nonetheless, about Cybil's steering Heidi to me and sharing our evening impressions. I'd seen what we had as private, but perhaps that was slipping away. I therefore felt resigned as I met with Heidi and the students--only three as it developed--and drove them with the equipment in a small maintenance truck. I parked as close as possible to the summit, but there was still a short rugged climb ahead. Heidi carried the refractor telescope and eyepiece sets, I the awkward reflector telescope and one of the mounts. The other mount I entrusted to Kirk, the only male student with us, who was also the lone male tennis player and the striker on our soccer team. I was struck by his versatility, though his papers in my class needed improvement.

"For maps and charts of the heavens we have smartphone apps," Heidi informed me. "Better than trying to read paper in the dark."

She got the telescopes set up and the students took turns viewing and working the adjustments. I had a few looks myself and was surprised at the closeness and clarity of the planets and their moons, the bringing to view of star clusters invisible to the naked eye. Heidi was encouraging and read data to me off her phone. After a time I felt good being out there, sharing some innocent pleasure with enthusiastic people, breathing the crisp night air. At the same time I felt apart from things, a visitor to the wondrous universe who hadn't achieved connection to its controlling force, its life-giving soul. Glancing over at Heidi, I saw someone claimed by others--particularly Jill--so that her company with me this night was strictly provisional. The students were apart from me by half a generation.

"There's something I wanted to mention to you," Heidi said softly.

"Oh?"

I sensed that it wasn't about astronomy, watched her glance back to check that the students were occupied.

"The thing is, I think you should know that Cybil, well, she has private meditation sessions with Makis."

"As his teacher, you mean?"

"That probably goes both ways, I think."

I didn't respond, turned my eyes to the sea. Heidi returned to her students. The way she had told me, so deliberately, suggested it was the real reason for my being there, on the outing. Cybil herself might have planned it, likely did. I waited stoically for interest in the stars to wane, helped again with the gear, drove everyone and everything back to the campus proper.

In the days and evenings that followed, I surprised myself by lurking in the shadows sometimes where I thought Cybil might be. I tried to appear casual due to the security cameras. My combined hope and fear was to discount or verify Heidi's allegation. Unfortunately, in my view, Cybil's absences from our beach rendezvous coincided exactly with visits by her to Great House. I tried not to show my disappointment when we met, wanting to retain even a strained relationship with her, but our shared yet unspoken awareness came to haunt our dusk meetings. There was a delicacy to each sunset, the spread of early stars, suggesting we had an illusion that might be shattered at any moment.

As for Makis himself, he seemed to be avoiding me. He continued to pop in at the other teachers' classes, being gregarious by nature, but he no longer appeared at mine. At times he would see me on campus but made no effort to approach or greet me. I considered that he might not like literature or, more likely, that he was dissatisfied with our soccer results, which so far consisted of an 0-6 record and being outscored 21-2. But there was no avoiding the greater, much more personal issue that divided us: Cybil, her sublimity and her affection.

At the start of soccer practice one day, Lucien informed me that Makis had suggested to him, rather strongly, a strategy to be used in our next game. It was our next-to-last for the season, the opponent

Queensbridge British School, one of the strongest among the private schools.

"He says pack the defense for the whole first half. No one goes past the center line for us except the striker. He wants to neutralize their speed and long passing, eliminate counter-attack and breakaway."

"What about the second half?"

"Then we loosen up. They'll be out of their game, he thinks, and our guys mostly rested. It'll even things out, he says, give us a chance."

"That'd be great but--I don't know, it seems to assume a lot."

"He says not to worry, he's sure it will work."

"Well, I guess we'll have to do it then. He's the boss."

"Yes, he's the boss."

I was rankled by Makis's communicating the plan to me through Lucien. It wasn't that he was afraid to face me, of course, so I saw it as an intentional slight. I wouldn't confront him on it because it was in the context of our soccer, which was only a game after all. But the message as to who was boss carried an implication that extended to our other--much more sensitive--shared interest. I had no idea how I would handle that.

We were accompanied to the game by Douglas, the instructor in economics and history, who was British and so had some interest in our opponent. It was an especially fine day and we enjoyed the added camaraderie on our ferry ride. The Queensbridge School gave us a friendly reception, an air of festivity pervading the larger than usual gathering of spectators. Douglas was acquainted with a few of them and did some socializing during our warm-ups. There was no sign of a referee until almost game time when a trio of them appeared. This was highly unusual for games at our level, the norm being only the center ref assigned from outside. The line refs were usually drawn from the onlookers, preferably one from each side, and would raise their flags only to mirror the center ref's calls.

"Any word over there on the flag men?" I asked Douglas.

"They have no idea, surprised as we are. And the fellows themselves speak only Greek, it seems."

The game began. It was nine against nine, my usual request being honored by the opposing coach. The home team was momentarily stalled by our packed defense, the ball cleared downfield on their first two attacks. The British boys adjusted quickly, however, their two forwards switching positions so that the stronger one was marked by our weakest defender, a flat-footed boy who could not keep up with his adversary. The Queensbridge forward was strongly built, aggressive, and emotional. He drove in to gain a clear shot, changing direction sharply on our player, the latter falling heavily trying to react. The attacker was eyeing the goal, poised to test our keeper with a smashing shot, when the sound of a referee's whistle brought play to a halt.

The center ref was shorter than the two on the lines, but severe and stubborn of countenance. He trotted up to where our player had fallen and was starting to get up, laid a hand on the boy's shoulder, and signaled our bench to attend to him. Lucien jogged out to have a look. He'd barely arrived, however, before the ref pivoted toward the strong Queensbridge forward and held a red card high in the air. The forward stood puzzled as the existing silence deepened, but only for a moment. Isolated shouts arose from the home team's sideline, then a general rumble of discontent. The forward showed anger as realization set it.

"Bloody barmy!" he shouted.

The ref pointed firmly toward the sideline and made a shooing gesture in the air. The ejected player reluctantly left as his teammates looked at each other aghast. Our player got up and seemed fine so Lucien returned to our sideline. The ref gave the scooping gesture to play on.

"Did our guy say he was hit?" I asked my assistant.

"Said nothing either way. He mostly seemed embarrassed."

We now had a nine to eight advantage in players but, true to Makis's strategy, we continued to pack the defense. Our opponents required two defenders and their keeper to prevent our striker, Kirk, from threatening their goal off a long feed. They therefore had only five players to attack eight defenders with their primary scorer gone. In addition, most of the foul calls went against them, warnings or yellow cards given when they tried more aggressiveness. Shortly before halftime, their disorganization allowed Kirk to make a run at their goal, but the keeper handily saved the shot.

"Another player with him," Lucien observed, "and we'd have a lead."

"Yes, but the boss is still the boss."

It appeared to me that the approach Makis had dictated was actually working. Our team was still competitive in the game and their morale was high for the second half. I gave them encouragement during the break as they sat or lay about on the grass, explained with Lucien how we'd open up when play resumed. Douglas stood silently at a distance, apparently sobered by events in the game, avoiding discussion of them with his friends across the field.

The opposing coach had made several substitutions to buoy his team's performance, so we were facing fresh legs. Due to our first half strategy, however, most of our players had done more standing than running, so fatigue was not a great factor. We had a second forward, Oscar, accompany Kirk downfield, and a midfielder float about the center circle to assist with opportunities. They were not long in coming, thanks in part to continued friendly calls by the referees. The Queensbridge defense became tentative, allowing Kirk to work a give-and-go with Oscar and slip a clothesline shot past the overmatched keeper. We had a lead! The home team understandably showed frustration, moving defenders and keeper up to bolster their depleted offense, limit the game to our side of the field. In their disjointed play, though, our floating midfielder found himself with the ball and lofted a long clearing kick that passed over the keeper's head and eventually trickled into their goal. The game was as good as over. Play deteriorated, tempers flared, the refs balancing their calls to maintain order. They quickly departed at game's end, the brawny linesmen flanking their smaller colleague.

"So what do you think?" I asked Lucien. "The officiating."

He shrugged.

"We caught a break. When you get them, you take advantage. It's part of the game."

Douglas had intended to stay for dinner with his friends, but instead returned with us on the ferry.

———⟋⟍⟍———

One of the kitchen workers brought a bottle of cognac next day to the men's cottage, compliments of Makis. It was accompanied by a short article from the English-language newspaper: "Tiny Island School Upsets Queensbridge." The headmaster was evidently in a celebratory mood, no doubt with a sense of vindication for past mistakes, and likely with greater optimism for the future. I was less certain of things myself, in fact drifting in the opposite direction. I had the obligatory drink with Lucien but then left for the shore to cogitate. I was somewhat surprised to find Cybil there.

"The days are getting shorter," she remarked. "Have to get here early for the sunset."

"Yes, and then the nights are colder."

We were silent for a time, watching the whitecaps, the sea more active than usual.

"Congratulations on your win," she said.

"Thank you." I hesitated, then: "I have some mixed feelings about it, actually. Doubts."

"Doubts?"

"The calls went quite heavily against them. Especially for a home team, and highly ranked."

"Well, that's not your problem, is it? Anyway, your team must have played well."

"I can't get away from thinking Makis had something to do with it."

She stared at me a moment, then turned to the reddening horizon.

"We have to remember we're deep in Europe here," she said. "It's not like back home, or even England."

"Yes, there aren't so many very rich men. One like Makis must have great personal power--controlling people, making events turn out to his liking."

"Isn't that what everybody would want if they had the money?"

"I don't know about everyone but--yeah, I guess most people."

We watched the orange-hued waves and heard them splashing against the boulders. Cybil is like those rocks, I thought, adamant in her ways.

"Your meditation," I resumed, "does all of this fit in with it? Makis, I mean, and his more or less philosophy, way of doing things."

"I wouldn't call it a philosophy," she said, "more like a method. A way to attain and honor quality by always seeking it, protecting it and passing it on. He won't ever have a philosophy course here, or sociology or religion. The idea is to avoid getting bogged down in abstractions, academic constructs, preachy ideals. He sees the most value in an ability and willingness to be fulfilled, as if it's an obligation, the real purpose of life. Things like self-sacrifice, self-denial, he considers evil, destructive of the quality in one's life, which is the only worthwhile ideal."

"And those who don't accept such thinking, are they also evil or worthless as individuals?"

Cybil appeared to reflect a bit.

"I don't know that he'd go that far, necessarily. I don't myself. There is a right to choose one's own path. People have the right to be wrong."

A chill breeze suddenly rose and she wrapped herself tightly in her sweater. The eastern horizon had gone dark.

"Ever think about leaving here?" I asked.

"No, not yet. I suppose I will eventually. I mean *we* will, Jill and Heidi and I. But for now he pays us so well, and we have no big expenses so we're saving most of it. For them it's a paradise, being here together and all. And for me, well, I feel involved with this place, at one with it, bonded."

"With Makis also?" I ventured.

She looked at me pointedly, then laughed as if deeply amused.

"Look!" she said turning away. "The first stars are out!"

The reportage on our soccer win was followed a day later by another, less welcome article: "Chicanery Alleged in Queensbridge Loss." Soon after, Lucien told me that the Independent Schools Association had notified Makis that St. Cyr Academy had forfeited our season-closing game against them. The nominal score of 3-0 in our favor would be recorded. This resulted in a final record for our team of 2-6 with our being outscored 21-7, normally considered poor but leaving Makis ecstatic. He looked forward to our closing success attracting attention to the school and boosting enrollment. His optimism was borne out in the following weeks, inquiries about mid-year or next-year transfers arriving steadily. The tainted nature of our profitable publicity faded into insignificance.

In my teaching I found that the student papers were not improving at all. Nor was the group's appreciation of literature, or even their interest in it. I asked the other teachers how the youngsters were doing in their classes, but got only the vaguest responses. It was apparently the progressive mode. When I pressed Jill on how she could possibly teach math without giving tests, she said she'd occasionally have a student do a problem on the blackboard, guiding him or her through it and hoping that something was learned. But she couldn't do it often because that would put pressure on the students, which was not progressive.

As the Christmas break approached, a schedule of teacher evaluations by Makis was distributed. My interview with the headmaster was listed in the bottom time slot. The day followed one of packing and departure for the students, our final day of work with them for the calendar year. I waited through the morning and afternoon as my colleagues successively traipsed to Great House for the tycoon's judgment. A chill wind whipped about the campus under a leaden sky. At the men's cottage window, I could easily imagine each lone teacher seated before the massive desk, Makis behind it indulging in his usual bombast. Darkness was already closing in by the time Douglas returned from his interview and said the headmaster was ready for me.

I found him as I'd imagined though not yet inclined to bombast.

He eyed me silently as I entered, then turned to open a lower desk drawer, chuckling a bit. A bottle of ouzo was produced along with two small glasses. He poured, gestured for me to join him in a drink. The other teachers had not mentioned or even hinted at this. The bottle remained on his desk.

"Great finish with the football," he said.

"Yes," I provisionally agreed. "I was hoping the boys could win one."

He quickly held up two fingers.

"Two! Superb effort doubly rewarded."

I smiled and nodded, as if modestly. He retrieved a cigar that had gone out and re-lit it. The surrounding smoke well suited his Zeus-like countenance and upper body.

"Did you enjoy it, then? Doing the football?"

"Oh, yes. More so at the end, of course."

Again the chuckle, deeper this time though overall he seemed restrained.

"Yes, it's always much better when you win."

He reached to one side and brought a manila envelope to center desk, the signal that we had business to discuss. Before opening it, however, he refilled his ouzo glass and topped mine off. Several smaller envelopes were then dumped out of the large one.

"The others," he said, "received their last payments for the term and modest bonuses. For you there is that also, but more."

He shoved two of the envelopes toward me, apparently done with them, and picked up one of the remaining two.

"This contains a lump-sum payment for your services through May, the end of second term, along with a grant of paid leave for that period."

I was silent, awaiting his explanation, but he was on to the remaining envelope.

"This is my letter of recommendation for you."

We stared at each other a moment.

"I'm afraid I don't understand."

"Actually, at some level, I think you do."

13

He drew over a thin folder that had lain under the large envelope, opened it, glanced at the sheets inside.

"The literature you had them read, your students, mostly seems on the airy side--Keats, Virginia Woolf, and such. Fine at other places, I suppose, maybe standard fare, but here we need some meat on the menu--Conan Doyle, Asimov, Louis L'Amour. Stuff like that."

"Genre fiction."

"Oh, not just fiction. But there's also the topics for their papers, political and especially social issues. But there's also the topics for their papers, political and especially social issues. Those are bottomless pits, Gordian knots that people waste their lives on. Personal progress requires communication skills--writing a good business letter, detailed proposal, marketing pitch."

I was stunned, didn't know what to say.

"Sorry if I disappointed you," I managed.

He seemed to relax, refilled his glass, held the bottle toward mine but I declined.

"I don't mean to be critical," he said. "It's just a question of how you fit at a place. If the fit isn't right, it's bad for both you and the place."

He wound up by saying he admired me as a person and certainly wished me well. We shook hands. I took the envelopes and exited Great House into the darkness and incongruous sleet.

⸻

I saw Cybil off at the ferry next morning, her friends waiting to board with her as we talked. They were leaving for a resort in Switzerland to which she gave me the address and directions, carefully printed out, her letters and digits reflecting the casual precision I'd come to know in her. I myself planned to leave on the ferry's return that afternoon.

"Come see us there," she said. "It'll be great fun!"

For a moment I pictured myself on a snowy mountainside with

14

the three women. Her invitation was purely pro forma, I saw. Had to be.

"I'll think about it," I responded.

She gave me a kiss on each cheek, European style. The contact was what I might expect from a sister or an aunt.

Later I visited what had been my classroom. I sat at the teacher's desk in front, faced the room with its ghosts, tried to meditate on my experience of the past few months. But in picturing Cybil, Makis, and the rest--the island, country, and continent--I sensed that I lacked the life experience, the mature perspective, to understand what had happened. I was capable of disappointment, and of disappointing, but I lacked the talent for coarseness that was apparently needed for strength, the power to adjust. I saw myself as a lightweight, a non-equal to the masters. I was distracted at this point by the sound of a maintenance man doing work in the building. He soon poked his head in and said he'd turned off the heat, I would soon be feeling cold. I sat on regardless, felt the cold as a sort of penance.

I lingered in Athens a few days upon leaving the island, but saw no point in remaining there. I also had no change of heart about Switzerland. I therefore returned to America and a hazy future, resolved only to make one more contact with Cybil to gain closure. People were still writing letters at the time, especially for international messages, so I wrote one to her at the school. I was thinking it might cause sadness, but I needn't have worried. Cybil sent me an upbeat response, revealing to my surprise that she was the school's new English teacher, meditation being lowered to club status.

TIMESHARE RENTAL

It had been a hard day for the car salesman, crazy customers who'd left his head spinning. He was glad he'd married a nurse, and a supervisor at that, with his own income shaky as the economy. She was in the kitchen now as he opened the back door of their split-level suburban home. A brochure and photos were spread on the table before her.

"What's all that?" Stuart asked by way of greeting.

"Margrit stopped by," Emily replied. "Left the info on Amaryllis Valley."

The salesman grunted on his way to the liquor cabinet.

"It looks really nice," his wife added, "and of course they'll discount us."

"You know I can't get the whole month. Larkin'll want me for the quota crunch. So two weeks tops."

"That's okay. Bob's cousin might take the rest if they don't strike on the Internet."

"I'm happy for them."

"So we're good with it then? Book the two weeks?"

"You mean we're serious on this?"

"Cut it out."

He took a long sip of whiskey.

"Yeah, go ahead. Hell with overthinking."

They escaped the metropolis on a cool Sunday, Stuart guiding their long sedan past full-blooming farmland, rolling hills and ridges, then the low mountains that showed shadowy blue from a distance. They had specific directions from Margrit and Bob, but those proved inadequate following a road closure for repair work. A detour was indicated but was poorly marked and confounding. A couple on horses finally told them they'd passed the turnoff far back.

"Easy to miss," the man said. "Just a weedy dirt road."

"Look for an old red mailbox," the woman added.

Stuart swung the car around and hit the gas.

"Makes one appreciate the suburbs," Emily said. "See? A benefit from our trip already."

"Just so it's not the highlight," Stuart responded.

The supposed dirt road was actually gravel, but had been either neglected or overused. The old trees hung heavily over to form a virtual cave. The road forked and would have posed another quandary but that Emily caught a glimpse of Amaryllis Valley through the brush. They were soon on a cindered driveway that skirted some well-spaced cottages above a placid lake. They continued for some distance, the big car raising billows of reddish-brown dust, until they reached one end of the lake and found number 22, their planned home for two weeks. Stuart parked next to the cottage and they stayed in the car awhile absorbing the rustic sounds, smells, and sunlight.

"I'm glad we came," he said.

"Great!" she responded, and rushed to give him a a kiss. "I knew you would be."

He smiled, then: "Well, let's get out."

As Emily began carrying things in, Stuart ambled to where he could better view their surroundings. They were located on a rise, the lake directly below them with a small beach. To the left a thick stand of trees cut them off from other properties. To the right about two hundred yards, downhill and forward with the curve of the lake, was a cottage about twice the size of their own. Beyond it was vacant land until across the water, where three cottages stood in close proximity to each other. The rest of the development was in the direction from which they'd come. A peaceful setting, Stuart thought, just what the doctor ordered.

But he suddenly heard voices, then laughter, rising from behind some bushes bordering the beach. A man and a woman emerged, sauntering towards the larger cottage. They were completely nude.

They sighted Stuart and waved, continued casually down the beach.

———※———

"They were wearing nothing at all?"

"Not a stitch."

"Margrit didn't say anything about it. Being that kind of place, I mean."

"Could be it's just them, not the place."

"Yes. There's weirdos popping up everywhere now."

They watched the other cottage as they had their small campfire that night, but it remained quiet and dark. Then, as they were preparing for bed, a car passed them on the cinder drive with laughter and shouts issuing forth. It continued down to the neighbors' place and was parked next to their SUV. Lights went on in the cottage and loud greetings were exchanged.

"Sounds like a late party," Stuart said. "We might be in for a long night."

But in less than half an hour there were exit sounds and the car went by again in the opposite direction, less noisily this time. Lights were extinguished in the big cottage. The night belonged to the owls and crickets.

"What do you make of it?" asked Emily in their bed.

"Well," Stuart answered sleepily, "It's like you said about weirdos."

———※———

The next morning, as Emily was dressing in their bedroom, a large inhuman face appeared at the window screen, staring at her and panting. Stuart was gone to get breakfast, so there was no use shouting. After a brief shock, Emily realized that the face was canine, but raised to an unnatural height since the window was rather high. She approached and expected to see a very large dog standing upright, paws against the outer wall. The animal, however, had all four feet on the ground, making it the biggest dog Emily had encountered. It had the general appearance of great Dane, but in a mix with something else, perhaps wolfhound.

"Upton!" someone female shouted. "Upton, get over here!"

The shouter, in shorts and sleeveless blouse, was languidly climbing the incline from the beach.

"Hello there," she spoke into the screen. "Sorry if he bothered you. I'm Eloise Pardo. We're your neighbors over there."

She gestured toward the larger cottage.

"Emily Wortham," Emily responded. "We just got in yesterday."

"Yes, I know. You renting from Bob and Margrit? Or did you buy them out?"

"Renting," Emily told her, "but just the first two weeks."

"Yeah? Who's coming after? Bob and Margrit?"

"No. I mean I don't know, but it won't be them."

"Oh, okay."

Emily judged her to be seven or eight years older than herself, past her season of discretion and falling into gracelessness. She was tall, blond hair tied back tightly, strangely pale for one who paraded nude in sunlight.

"So," Eloise continued, "what do you do? You and your husband?"

Emily hesitated, irritation encroaching.

"You mean our work? Our jobs?"

"Yes."

"Well, I'm a nurse. Stuart's in car sales."

The other woman smiled brightly.

"No kidding! Ashton's a wholesaler, does cars sometimes."

Emily assumed that Ashton was the man with her. Husband?

"Oh," she responded.

Eloise waited for more. Emily simply smiled.

"Well, come on, Upton. Let's get going." Then, as they moved away: "We'll invite you for barbecue!"

Hope it rains that day, Emily thought. Watching them go, she noticed that, despite Upton's size and likely appetite, Eloise carried neither poop-scoop nor baggie.

———

With the day's rising heat, the Worthams decided to test the lake water for a swim. It was cold, Emily hesitating at knee depth, Stuart plunging all-in to adjust quickly. He decided to swim to the opposite shore with its three clustered cottages. Emily watched as he splashed off, strongly at first, slowing before he'd gained the bottom. Was he all right? He was swimming back towards her without his previous energy. She looked up at the three cottages, but they were quiet and lifeless as ever.

"Water snake," Stuart explained.

"Are they dangerous?"

"Don't know. There's different kinds, I suppose."

He looked up the lake through the greater part of Amaryllis Valley. In the distance a woman played with children in the shallows, an inept kayaker well beyond. No real swimming was going on.

"It seems we're being watched," Emily said.

He followed her line of vision to where Ashton Pardo stood in the shade beyond his cabin, Upton lying near him.

"Thanks for the warning, fella," Stuart said.

"Oh, now. It isn't like we've officially met him."

"All it takes is a shout. Unless he doesn't give a damn, or even--"

"Now, Stuart. We shouldn't prejudge."

"Well, with what we've seen and heard so far, it's not exactly a 'pre.'"

Emily decided to let it rest. They returned to their cottage to shower and plan their evening. Mr. Pardo was ignored.

They'd had a pleasant time at the Viking Supper Club, a quality buffet dinner and entertainment by local musicians. Their moods were rejuvenated and they again felt good about their vacation. The roads were very dark on their return, especially the cinder driveway, where a mother deer and baby forced Stuart to brake hard. Reaching their cottage, they saw that the Pardos had a male guest with whom they conversed around a fire. He was a younger man and did most of the talking.

"Let's get to bed before they invite us down," Emily suggested.

She got her way and was lying in satisfied bliss when suddenly she was awakened by discordant shouting from the big cottage. She crept to the window and peeked out, saw the fire was gone but lights were on inside. She could distinguish two male voices, one deeper than the other, and Eloise trying to mediate, ineffectively. Glancing back at the bed, Emily saw Stuart still slumbering, having imbibed more than she at the Viking. She would have to adjust to this on her own. Deciding that the night had cooled enough, she quietly closed the window and returned to bed.

Stuart was still asleep when dawn broke, so Emily reopened the window to give him a nice fresh breath of morning. The only sounds now were those of nature, so much more pleasant, but Emily noticed that Upton was on a long leash tied to the Pardo cottage, apparently unattended. The couple's SUV was gone, a European sports car near its place. All windows and doors of the cottage were shut.

As she was preparing breakfast, Emily heard a distant screen door slamming, Stuart stirring from bed, then his subdued laughter.

"She was wearing panties this time," he said as he came out. "Gave the dog a dish."

"You mean Eloise?"

"Yeah, she's getting decent."

"And maybe richer. You saw the different car?"

"No, I didn't notice."

"And you in car sales. A super-expensive import, and it's red."

"Wow. Guess I need my coffee."

———※———

Walking along the cinder driveway, they found many of the cottages unoccupied, the clubhouse locked and unattended, a mother and child by themselves at the playground. She confirmed the existence of the water snakes, didn't know the Pardos, said she was there free as a gift from her boss. Eloise and Stuart walked on as the heat rose in earnest. They found a kayak beached with male clothing draped over it to dry. Stuart viewed it silently, felt himself perspiring and his mood changing.

"Let's go back the way we came," he said.

"But we're halfway round," Emily responded. "Why not see the other side?"

"That rough stretch ahead. Too woody. Bugs and all, more snakes."

Emily acquiesced. It was no big deal. They returned to their cottage and she made lemonade. They were relaxing in the shade of a huge elm when suddenly Ashton Pardo appeared in a state of restrained anxiety.

"Another hot one, eh?"

"Sure seems that way," Stuart responded.

"I'm your neighbor. Over there."

He gave a head tilt in the known direction. He was below average height for a man, Emily saw, perhaps shorter than his wife, and of indefinite age. She rose from her chair as they exchanged names.

"Let me get you a lemonade."

"That'll be great. Thank you."

He drew up a third chair next to Stuart, closer than Emily's.

"Here for the whole month?" he asked.

"No, just a couple weeks."

"Good two weeks for getting away. The hottest, probably. Great time to ditch the city awhile."

"We're out in the 'burbs, actually. Home and work."

Pardo grunted. Stuart felt instinctive dislike for him, unreasonable maybe but it was there, just as with some of his customers. But that gave him practice in controlling it, as he wanted to now for the sake of Emily and their vacation trip.

"Eloise mentioned you're in auto sales."

"Yes, that's right."

"I handle them wholesale, along with assorted other items."

"What other items?"

Stuart hoped to shut off any prying by someone he didn't like. Pardo showed a flicker of irritation at the sudden distraction.

"Oh, many things. Household items, lingerie, coffee--"

"Coffee! Now *that* must be interesting. Mostly imported, I suppose."

"Yes," the other man responded slowly, then: "as are the bulk of autos I deal with."

Emily returned with Pardo's lemonade and an additional snack table. She resumed her seat on Stuart's other side. She'd noticed that the visitor was leaning toward her husband as if intent on something. She would just listen, she decided.

"When I heard you're in auto sales," Pardo continued, "well, I don't mean to mix pleasure with business but it gave me an idea. See, I happen to have a trailer of high-enders I'm looking to liquidate below wholesale. It's to finance a time-sensitive investment. One of them is parked next to our SUV. You maybe noticed it, the Aston Martin."

"Hard to miss," Stuart said. "A real beauty."

"Right. And the other eight on the trailer are just as snazzy. There'd be huge profits for you selling them retail, and they'd surely go fast. My head detailer brought this one in last night. He can have all nine ready to go soon as you do the bank transfer."

"Whoa! Hold on a sec, Pardo. I don't have a free-standing lot. I work for a new car dealership. Our *used* car department is mostly trade-ins."

"Mostly, right. But no used car manager will pass up a great deal.

Call your UCM and give him the low-down. I'm sure he'll jump at the opportunity. And you'll look great for steering it to them."

Stuart hesitated, glanced at Emily.

"I don't know," he began skeptically.

"Excuse me," Emily said getting up. "I have to check in the cottage."

She left them to discuss business, not exactly her forte.

"Where did you pick these cars up?" Stuart asked Pardo.

"Different places. Auctions, contacts, individual owners."

"Salvage jobs?"

"Not that I'm aware of."

"Titles all clear?"

"No, we took them on surety bonds. That helps us get them low. You can establish title later, having the time and all."

Stuart considered this, pictured himself asking the UCM to expend a quarter to half a million dollars for used car inventory.

"How do you happen to have this many at once?"

"It was for a specialist dealer in the South. Buys in bulk for his sales events. He had the surety bonds checked out, found one of them bad. It was my head detailer's contact, he should have caught it. Blew the whole deal. All nine cars sent back."

"And you refunded him?"

Pardo cowered, seemed to shrink into himself.

"That's pending, let's say." A hesitation, then: "His payment had been used on that investment I mentioned."

And so, Stuart thought, unload the cars on Stuart.

"You can't get a refund on the investment?"

"It's an outfit in Columbia."

I won't ask if it's coffee, Stuart told himself, I'll presume for the record that it is.

"Look," Pardo pressed, "you don't have to sell the UCM on all nine. Just the eight that pass muster. Keep the Aston for yourself, for free! A gift from me for greasing the deal."

Stuart didn't respond, looked away from the other's desperate face to the sizzling lake surface with snakes swimming below. The three cottages on the other side looked very peaceful, their timeshare holders in distant locales, secure and safe from the wiles of the man sitting next to him.

———※———

The Worthams lingered over a late lunch, savoring the absence of their intrusive neighbors. Emily was perplexed by the proposed deal, as Stuart had described it, happy that he'd refused but annoyed that such matters could pursue them on vacation. The priority of business had always bugged her.

"Did you want to seek local attractions today?" she asked.

"I don't know, we're pretty well through the day, plus it's a scorcher."

"Yes. They said on the radio tomorrow will be better. The nature reserve is really beautiful, according to Margrit, and there's two railroad museums, one life-size and one models. The cheese factory serves lunch, might be worth a try."

Stuart gazed out the window, expressionless.

"Sure. Whatever you like."

Emily studied him.

"You seem rather pensive. Is it still the proposal?"

"No, not exactly. But, well, do you think I might become like him? A hustler? A shady dealer? We're in similar fields, after all. Overlapping. I've seen guys something like him in sales, just less extreme. But maybe on their way."

"No," Emily answered firmly. "You're nothing at all like him. You're an honest working man."

She took his hand, would have kissed him but for the table.

"Thanks," he responded, and covered her hand with his free one.

"Want to stay in for dinner later?" she asked.

"Yeah, that'll be fine. I'll open the pinot grigio."

———※———

Fire in the night.

It registered at once in Emily's consciousness as she woke to the dancing orange glare opposite their bedroom window. She crept to the window fearfully, not thinking to wake Stuart who was in wine-assisted oblivion. She saw the Pardos' cottage ablaze--raging intensity throughout--with Upton on his leash tied to a tree. A few onlookers were arriving, keeping distant from both fire and dog. A distant siren wailed.

The mortal terror brought to mind something Emily had heard on local radio the day before. A man's body had been found in a ditch between their resort and the town. She'd been interested in the weather forecast, then in Stuart's talk with Pardo and in making plans, so the news story was forgotten. Could it have something to do with Pardo's absence that morning and the argument of the previous night? But then she felt Stuart's hand on her shoulder as he peered past her.

"What the hell," he said.

"Yes, hell it is."

A fire engine arrived but there were no hydrants, so the firemen focused on controlling Upton. The flaming cottage was unapproachable. Stuart and Emily went outside and saw a large man in chief's helmet standing with hands on hips. He was eyeing the Pardo SUV, as yet little damaged, perhaps considering how to rescue it. The Aston Martin was gone.

"Excuse me," Emily addressed the chief, "I'm a nurse. Can I be of any help?"

"Not to anybody in there," he gestured. "But stick around. One or two of the boys might need you after this tussle."

He was distracted by one of the firemen returning to their vehicle.

"Gotta use the dart gun!" the man called. "He's too big!"

The chief left to prep the tranquilizer. Emily stood with Stuart as the fire raged unabated.

"What do you make of it?" she asked.

"A real inferno," he frowned, "all through the place. And I guess it was sudden. Could be an accelerant was used."

"What about the sports car gone? The dog tied up outside? In the middle of the night?"

"Suspicious, yeah. I dunno, you got any ideas?"

Emily related the radio news story.

"Ah," Stuart reacted, "this is getting pretty heavy. Still some questions, though. The Pardos didn't seem up to all this."

"Well, you never know about people. Especially under stress."

"Yes, that's true."

They watched as Upton was pacified and the fire engine's on-board water was dispensed, wetting down the SUV and surrounding plant life. A police car and ambulance arrived and, after some discussion, Upton was loaded into the ambulance. The fire continued to light the night but declined from its peak intensity. Emily and Stuart retreated to their cottage.

———⟨⟨———

The morning was overcast and humid, the acrid smell of burnt lumber hanging stubbornly in the air. Emily stepped around their cottage to view the ruin below. The first responders and onlookers were gone, a man in coveralls and one in a suit poking about in the embers. The man in suit noticed her and came up the incline showing a detective badge. They introduced themselves.

"Was anyone in there?" she asked him.

"It doesn't appear so. We've found no remains. Do you know the people staying there or where they might be?"

"No. We've just been here a couple days. They were total strangers to us."

He nodded and looked away, disappointed Emily thought.

"You or your husband see anything, hear anything before the fire? Anything suspicious?"

"No, I'm afraid not. This is a total shock to us. We were looking forward to a nice, peaceful vacation."

"Yes, I can imagine. Where's your husband now, by the way?"

"Sleeping in. He had a little wine last night, then with the interruption, well, he's making up for it."

"Right. Well, thanks for your time, ma'am. We don't have the tape with us, but no one should touch the debris until we finish our investigation. It's still real hot in some places."

"Okay, I'll pass that on."

Later, when Stuart was up, they agreed there was no point in staying at Amaryllis Valley. They would pack up and spend the coming night at a motel in town. Then, rested from the hectic night before and the sickening smoke smell, they'd drive back to their sane suburban neighborhood.

"Maybe I can get us a refund," Emily suggested.

"Don't worry about it," Stuart rejoined. "Just getting away will settle things fine."

———

Back in their air-conditioned split-level, Stuart relaxed with an iced whiskey while Emily phoned Margrit from the adjoining room. He waited, expecting his wife to give her friend what for, but Emily had hardly spoken before she too was just a listener. Stuart sat puzzled and sipping. When the phone conversation had ended, Emily came in and sat staring at Stuart blankly.

"So what gives?" he inquired.

"More like given," she replied, "or else just dumped. A red Aston Martin, sitting in their driveway when they got up this morning. Keys in the mailbox."

Stuart took some time to absorb this: the problem car, reason for Pardo's approach to him, inducement for him--Stuart--to cajole his UCM into buying the other eight, none with titles.

"I guess they got Margrit and Bob's address from some records about the time shares," Emily continued. "Mistook it for ours."

"They?" Stuart mused.

"Yes. I mean someone--the Pardos, people Ashton dealt with, whoever."

"Whoever, yes. I guess it doesn't matter. The result is the same."

He envisioned the trailer truck pulling up to the dealership he worked for, cash on delivery expected for the luxury vehicles on board. A conversation would ensue, turning heated, perhaps with profanities, threats. There might well be police involvement.

"What is it, Stuart? What are you thinking?"

"The thing is," he responded, "I can't remember clearly how I left it with Pardo. I remember the heat, the glare off the lake, my mind sort of dreamy, wandering, him still talking. I don't know exactly what he was saying, or what I said back. I just wanted to be rid of him, so I said whatever would do the trick."

Emily took some time to respond, Stuart glancing up sheepishly at her.

"Well," she said, "it seems the trick was on us."

"Yeah," he acknowledged. "But then it was from the beginning, right?"

Emily got up to go call the police. Stuart sat sipping whiskey, gazing out their living room window at nothing in particular.

White Sands

"Happy 1970, Tim."

The Malay woman gave me a smile as she left the office with her work friend. The rhinestones in her white eyeglass frames sparkled from the overhead lights. Exactly fifty years later, she'd be giving her last New Year's greetings.

———

Not far into the new year I supplanted the work friend in driving Mila around. We took our breaks and lunches together, she the talker and I the listener. She'd unload on me about her supervisor, the clerks, and her clients.

"You're my confidante," she said.

I've never been sure what attracted us to each other, but it was there in our initial looks, the tone of our mundane greetings. It became understood in the office that we were a couple, a union somehow of contrasting appearances and personalities. She charmed some people and aggravated others, sunny or stormy by turns, petite but uninhibited in her new land. With me she was simply calm and friendly.

———

With the coming of warm weather, Mila departed the office for another job. She also left the apartment she'd shared with three other women and took a room with shared bathroom in a converted old house. I could visit her there, but we were more comfortable on the front steps, viewing and hearing the city summer night. Her sporty new car was parked on the street. She didn't drive it much, but she enjoyed having it, keeping it clean and sparkling under the streetlights.

I was in my own first apartment then, an old-fashioned studio in a Victorian building abutting the lake shore. We went there once on a Saturday after walking in a nature reserve. She'd looked especially beautiful that day, standing before the forest backdrop with a light wind in her hair. In the apartment she rested on my bed, smoothing her dress under her and closing her eyes. After a time I approached her and we kissed. It was unexpected yet we weren't surprised.

"Take the PACE test, Tim."

"Why?"

It was the exam for federal employment.

"We can work together again."

"I might be assigned elsewhere."

"Anyway, it will be better for you."

But I'd already made a move I considered more important. I'd entered a master's degree program to raise myself to Mila's educational level. The courses fit my work schedule, so I considered it an obvious step in building our relationship.

———

The eve of New Year's 1971 found us in a studio apartment Mila had taken, an upgrade with its own bathroom. We sat before her small television awaiting the celebrations. We were on the floor, knees up, she with her back against me as if I were her chair. I loosely held her, the moment one of casual intimacy that was becoming infrequent for us. The master's program demanded more of my time than I'd foreseen. Still, it seemed to be necessary and we were still close.

There came a ringing of the doorbell, odd considering the hour. Mila ignored it but the ringing persisted. She told me it was one of her countrymen, married with children, angry because she'd spurned him. It was bitterly cold outside where he was standing, so she got up and buzzed him in. He came up the short flight of steps and stood shivering within the apartment door. He was smoking a cigarette despite his being a doctor. They exchanged a few statements in their own language and he left. He'd seemed a good enough sport and I wondered what it more exactly concerned. Mila did not explain further, however, only saying that the man was childish.

With the return of warm weather, Mila developed an illness. She moved to a sister's flat on the upper floor of a large old house on a quiet side street. The nature of the illness was vague, but she spent a great amount of time in bed and had taken a leave from her job. She looked about normal to me when I visited, but I'd only speak with her briefly since the sister was always present and Mila, I was told, needed to rest a lot. The sister was taller and strikingly attractive in appearance. Mila seemed to encourage our socializing with each other, though both the sister and I held back.

It turned out that a relationship had developed between Mila and a man in the federal office where they worked. The bed-confining illness occurred simultaneously. Rather than impinge on their contacts, however, the malady became the man's chance to shower Mila with attention, thus ingratiating himself with her. She was taken by surprise and duly impressed.

"He carried me," she reported over the phone.

I rarely saw her in person then, given the situation, and the phone calls were usually hers. There came a gap in our communication until she called excitedly one night and told me she'd gotten married.

It should have been the end of things between Mila and me, our story joining those of my other short-lived friendships, but in fact it was more like a beginning. Her calls to me resumed after an interval in which she'd become disillusioned. The husband's efforts to please her had virtually ended, the strength he'd shown at work now seen as habitual coarseness. There were frequent arguments, escalating in their intensity, and he was not above intimidation. Once again I became Mila's confidante.

I'd continued in my master's program even after her marriage defeated its purpose. I was more han halfway through, saw it might have other uses, and had more vacant time since losing Mila. With her new difficulties, I was again involved with her, but not on a demanding level. I was also writing my thesis rather than taking courses, which allowed me greater flexibility. When Mila managed a transfer to escape working with her husband, I was able to visit her at a small satellite office. It seemed to be something that was always meant to happen.

⁓

"So, now you are a Master of Arts."
"On paper, anyway."
We were in a coffee shop in the mall enclosing her office.
"Will you look for a better job?"
"Yes. The degree is mostly for teaching, of course."
"My old vocation."
"There aren't so many openings just now. The counselor only found me one. In New Zealand."
"Oh, close to my homeland."
"You think we should go there? Just dump everything here?"
She looked out over the shop, the mall outside, smiled.
"No, I don't think so."

⁓

I was loafing in my apartment one evening when she called and sounded upset.
"We were in the car," she said, "going to a family party. I wore

a nice dress, I had a gift, and then he starts complaining and says he doesn't want to go. We start arguing and he turns the car around and comes back. Now here I am again, back in my bed. I still have my nice dress on."

"Why didn't he want to go?"

"He hates some of the men there. They joke him about not having a baby yet. They ask if he wants them to show him how."

"Is he there with you now?"

"No. He brought me in and then went out by himself. He slammed the door. He's off somewhere being mad. I don't care about him."

"Sounds pretty bad. Will you be all right there, do you think?"

"Oh, he'll want to make up, especially when I talk about divorce. He grabs me then and hugs me and says we can't ever get divorced, then more hugs and with kisses."

"And you wind up going along with him."

"Yes. He's so pathetic that I give in. It would be so different if we weren't married. Just leave him then. But divorce is difficult. Marriage is like a prison."

———⟋⟍———

There were person-to-person selling clubs that were popular at the time, cosmetics and housewares and such. Mila joined one that pushed nutritional drink powders. It afforded her more absence from her husband, pleasant contacts with customers, and of course visits to me. I always bought a canister of the powder to legitimize our meeting, a sort of joke between us. She later switched to selling jade jewelry, which I'd buy as gifts for my family, but not on every visit since it was more costly. Soon she simply dropped the selling when she came.

I'd moved to the building where the doctor had interrupted our New Year's Eve. She liked this, our common choice of residence, and felt at home. We became physically intimate. One Saturday afternoon the phone rang during our intimacy. When I answered, an incoherent voice on the other end expressed anger. I assumed it was a friend of mine who jested this way, and so I answered light-heartedly. The caller responded that he wasn't my friend and that I knew who he was. I did not yet, however, and dismissed him with a flippant remark. I was getting many crank calls at the time.

"That was him," Mila informed me.

"Oh? How did he get my number?"

"He goes through my things. He's an asshole."

"I see."

We hadn't seen much need for caution in the years of our relationship. To the world's eyes we were simply friends from a job who had stayed in contact. It might have become an issue now except, a month or so after the intrusive phone call, Mila told me she was pregnant. I walked her to her car after that meeting, a fine drizzle accentuating an unusual city silence. As she maneuvered out of her parking space, then pulled away, I felt an overwhelming sympathy for her. And encroaching helplessness.

The child, a boy, was born in early summer. Mila and I had little contact during the pregnancy, but she had ample support from her relatives. Her husband retreated into silence. His family was happy at the prospect of his fatherhood, but Mila could see that he harbored suspicion. She'd considered abortion early on, I giving no opinion, the idea fading amid the ebullience of others. She asked me to visit her and the baby at a relative's apartment, and to hold him. I kept the appointment and accepted the little person from a teenage cousin of Mila's who was assisting with his care. The two women looked back and forth between the baby and me, as if searching for resemblance. I myself felt a vague mixture of emotions, paramount among them a desire to hand the child back to the cousin.

I didn't see the child or Mila for a couple of years after that, though she occasionally called me. She'd ask about my early medical history, relating it to her son's development, her husband's history deemed irrelevant. She also didn't trust him with the child. There was an incident of tea in the baby bottle, leading to an emergency room visit. At least once the tiny boy had been dropped. There was a carelessness or lack of sensitivity that, in Mila's view, stemmed from her husband's doubts about paternity. The use of DNA testing for this was still a decade off.

When I eventually saw her again it was in their suburban home. I felt somewhat like an intruder, though it was by Mila's invitation with the spouse away. The boy had turned two, was silent and passive, abruptly falling asleep in our presence. When Mila and I moved to another room, he suddenly awoke crying as we were becoming intimate. I visited again a couple of weeks later at a similarly safe time. The boy was more active but his actions were undirected, apparently motiveless. He walked stiffly about in different directions, eyeing me curiously, then grew tired or bored and curled into unconsciousness. Mila and I moved carefully out and this time were not interrupted.

The child's slow development became an issue of sorts, a shadow over our relationship. There was nothing in either of our histories to account for it, so questions arose about his early care, particularly by Mila's husband. The man grew angry at any reference to this, and Mila was limited in what she could tell the pediatrician. A grudging and delicate tolerance came to rule their household.

The cold stasis in Mila's marriage extended into the 1980s, so I became marginalized in her life. I naturally became involved with other women but increasingly found the lifestyle tedious. I married somewhat impulsively at one point in the succession, became a legal father, and found myself enmeshed in demands that replaced premarital interests. One fresh spring day, however, I stopped with my wife and small son at a large park and there ran into Mila. She was sitting on a bench watching one of her brothers play with her son, now almost six. Introductions were done. She gave no hint of our relationship, the brother showing no awareness of it. Little was said before her son took off in a sudden sprint across the park, his uncle in difficult pursuit. Mila watched with some concern.

"He does that sometimes. He's very fast."

We left her on the bench, I sensing a tiredness on her part. Her son had been silent, perhaps still non-verbal, while her brother filled the vacant paternal role. This would be the last time I'd see her in person.

When the Internet came into being, I sometimes sought updates on the lives of people I'd known, including Mila. Nothing much was posted for her beyond changes of address with eventual separation from her husband. Strangely, there was nothing at all about her son, even when he'd have reached adulthood. Mila's last name changed and, on researching her apparent second husband, I found that he was twenty years younger than her, a doctor and compatriot. This led me to recall a story from her past that she'd told me as her "confidante." As still a student and prior to her emigration, she'd had a crush on an older man, a business associate of her father's. She had a breakdown when the man relocated, tearfully watched his plane leaving. Her family had her stay at a resort to recover.

"It was my beautiful summer," she said. "There were the white sands, the ocean breezes, and the lovely music in the evenings."

In comparing the ages of Mila and the man whose name she now shared, I saw he could be other than a husband to her: an earlier son resulting from her naiveté with the businessman. She'd have assisted the adult son with immigration, assumed his last name to reflect their relationship, thankfully discarding that of her ex-husband.

Having reached my conclusion about Mila's younger man--that he was the outcome of her very early romance--I flagged in my attention to her. When I finally saw a new posting about her, it was her obituary. She had died several months previous during the first year of the Covid-19 pandemic. I recalled being told by my ex-wife at that time about a phone message for me on her machine. She was unable to make out many details, but someone referred to as my "former friend" had passed away. The male caller spoke rapidly in a rather harsh voice.

The online obituary listed her current husband, the man twenty years her junior, as the lead survivor. He was followed by Mila's son, her ex-husband as a dear friend, and about a dozen siblings with their spouses. One sibling was predeceased--the very attractive sister in whose home I visited Mila during her illness. I was not mentioned, of course, though someone had known enough to make that call.

"You won't come running after your son, will you?" Mila had said.

I'd strictly followed her wishes, had not found it difficult, but she herself perhaps had let something slip.

There was a picture of her next to the text, her face and shoulders. She was smiling and radiant, turning toward the camera, wearing a lacy white dress. It was hard to tell her age. There was a link to a gallery of more pictures, which I clicked. Only a few were from when she was young. There were a couple of vintage photos from before her emigration, and a couple more of her holding her son as a preschooler. She looked happy but with hints of stress. The rest of the pictures were from recent years, showed her in groups of relatives and friends, and they left me stunned. She was hardly recognizable. Her face had deep vertical creases, seeming to evince a downward pull on her mouth and eyelids. She wore bulky clothing, giving her a generally shapeless look, her posture suggesting a beaten-down fragility. It was a transformation that for me was not explained by age alone.

The son was also in a few later pictures. He was tall and bore no resemblance to Mila, contrasting sharply with the Malay men around him. He wore jeans and sweatshirt and once a cardboard crown from a fast-food restaurant. His expression was vacant, too disinterested to be confused, and I sensed a cognition issue.

I later considered whether I should have intervened, courted Mila more tenaciously before the first husband controlled her life. It might have shut off the destructive pressure and conflicts that followed. She eventually found solace in the young doctor, but the prime of her life was not at all what it should have been.

———

I drove to the doctor's clinic and parked within view of the entrance. I watched people enter and exit, debated whether to keep my appointment for an annual wellness visit. My plan was to say I was a widower, rather than divorced, leading him to acknowledge that he was one also. From there I might inquire about Mila, her later life and degree of suffering. The doctor might not tell me much, my pose as a stranger not helping, but anything at all would assist my understanding, help me toward closure.

Sitting in the car, however, I came to see what I was doing as something just for myself. Mila was gone and I could no longer help her. The chances I'd had were buried in the distant past. The doctor might be hurt by my fishing for details, having made his own adjustment, especially if he saw through my subterfuge. If news of my interest were to reach Mila's son, it could cause great confusion and further hurt. It was exactly what she'd wanted to avoid. Even though Mila was gone, I was bound to keep my promise to her.

I started my car, took a last look at the clinic, and pulled away down the street. This would have to be my closure: the acceptance of an ending, as Mila had accepted hers in the year of her beautiful summer.

I was finally on her level.

THE SECLUDED LITERATUS

Faith had been quite some time in her father's bedroom, so Lyle was stuck watching the nature show alone. It was the best they could do, he knew, given how his and her lives had gone. And Dad kept hanging on, a drain on their relationship from the beginning, Faith even doing the crosswords with him to keep his brain functioning. But yeah, it was Dad's house and he, Lyle, had made decisions over many years that had landed him here. He was lucky, actually, to have hooked up with Faith after the decades of disaster with Mary Ellen. He and Faith were a couple far past their primes, he especially, but at least they had this haven, mortgage-free thanks to Dad. He was a bother but, truth be told, they had no better place to go.

A tiny creature on the TV show puffed himself up and danced to attract a mate. Lyle laughed out loud and reached for his wine glass. It was virtually empty. He raised it to his mouth anyway and tipped it, collected a drop or two. He glanced over at Faith's glass, still brimming with pinot grigio. He was tempted.

Why, he wondered, is it taking so long? Go to sleep, old boy. Be done with it.

He resisted the temptation and got to his feet, took the four steps to their front screen door, achieved his escape from educational broadcasting.

Standing on the concrete stoop, hands on hips, he surveyed the familiar scene. Their modest house was the last on this side of the street, which dead-ended into a high cyclone fence to his right. Beyond the fence was a large tract of weedy land belonging to a convent some distance off. Across the street was the side of a property belonging to Ben, a widower with an attractive daughter who would sunbathe in the back yard before the cyclone fence. Between that yard and the back of Ben's house was a three-car garage with its doors opening onto the street. The house itself, a barn-like structure, faced another side street that branched off Lyle's. The dead end was thus bordered by a side of Ben's property and the three houses that faced it. This odd bit of street had never been paved by the city, only receiving some occasional pea gravel courtesy of Ben or Faith's father. Deep ruts had been formed by stuck vehicles, particularly those driven by Ben's boarders, to whom he rented his excess space.

The prairie beyond the fence had been put up for sale by the nuns, but a potential buyer had ordered a foreboding geological survey. The shallow depression in its center that was a pond after rainstorms was judged to signify a potential giant sinkhole. Not only did the field not sell, but the market values of neighboring properties fell precipitously.

The house next to Dad's was little more than a shack, someone's do-it-yourself project from decades past. The inhabitants hung their wet laundry right next to Dad's driveway. Lyle would thus have their underwear and socks in his face when he stood at the kitchen sink. The adults had two boys they'd adopted for state subsidies, one of whom had pelted Lyle's car with eggs, he believed.

Lyle sat down on the top cement stair. He'd once have had a quiet evening smoke in this position, but now smoking and his youth were just faded memories. Faith had displaced his entire earlier life, mostly for the better, though sometimes there were sudden reminders. This very evening, before she'd changed the channel, he'd been watching news coverage of some rioting downtown, inner-city youths smashing windows and looting, starting fires. They were descendants of people to whom he'd issued Public Aid, grandparents and great-grandparents of the looters. It was worthwhile work, he and his colleagues had told themselves, morally superior to business and the professions. It coincided with the many new programs then purporting to seek social justice. Well, things hadn't worked out, Lyle saw, had in fact gone the other way. He'd come to feel shame, almost guilt, for having been part of it, and for bypassing a quality career that was his natural destiny. His graduate degree in literature had gathered dust for decades as he attempted escape into real estate, then restaurant management. Bankruptcy and divorce were the fruits of his labors until he finally found Faith.

"I've refreshed your wine," came her voice from behind.

He got up and went inside.

"Get tired of the animals?" she asked.

"Had to stretch my legs. You were back there quite a while."

She sipped from her glass. He took a larger drink from his. When she didn't speak, he looked over and saw she was staring blankly at the darkening picture window.

"Something wrong?"

She hesitated a moment before responding.

"Dad passed away."

Her statement hung in the air between them, a low-wattage lamp in the far corner their only light.

"Just now was it?"

"No. A half hour ago, maybe longer. Say forty minutes."

"You're sure he's--ah, gone?"

"He stopped breathing. There's no pulse."

"Did you listen at his chest for a heartbeat? Feel it?"

"No. I didn't, no."

She drank absently from her wine, looking past him into space.

"I'll go do it," he said, and got up.

The elderly man was in bed in the master bedroom. His eyes were closed and mouth slightly open. A club chair was pulled up next to him, no doubt where Faith had been sitting. Lyle pulled down the covers a bit and put his ear to Dad's chest, listening through thin pajamas. There was no sound or pulsation. Lyle straightened and gazed through a bedroom window over the now moonlit field toward the distant convent, a place of prayer and reflection. Yes, he mused, this was a dead man, but what now? His eyes fell to the bedside table, amber prescription bottles and a glass that had held diluted cranberry juice, Dad's habitual nightcap. He'd recently been leaving about half of Faith's serving, but this night there was only a trace. The medications seemed fewer also. Inspecting the bottles, Lyle found the blood thinner and two other heart medications, but no sign of the pain reducer or the aid for sleeping.

Lyle returned to the living room.

"You're right," he told Faith. "He's dead."

"So call the funeral home?"

"Won't they be closed now? This late?"

"They might be having a wake. Or embalming someone."

"Oh, yeah. Well, I guess it should be you. Immediate family and all."

He stayed on the couch drinking wine while she talked on the kitchen phone. Something about the conversation didn't sound right. Too impersonal, then too brief.

"I got their answering service," Faith informed him. "I said it was an emergency. She said I'd get a call back."

They waited ten, fifteen, twenty minutes in near silence. Lyle finished his wine. Faith noticed and finished hers also.

"We got anything stronger?" Lyle asked, pointing at his glass.

"Dad's old brandy. Cabinet over the fridge."

He went and got it, a bottle almost full. He brought the wine out also in case Faith wanted to stay with it. But she declined both beverages, fixated on the coming call, until finally the phone did ring. Lyle sipped brandy as Faith talked in the kitchen, her voice faltering as the funeral director responded at length. On her return she sat down demurely and poured herself wine.

"He says we should have called first responders."

"What, like for an emergency?"

"Yes. He's doing it himself now."

"So they'll be coming here with lights flashing and sirens and all?"

"I guess so. Like on TV maybe."

"What the hell for? He's been dead a long time now."

"I don't know. Some procedure they have to do before the funeral home gets the body. A police report, a death certificate, stuff signed by officials."

"Oh, yeah. The death certificate. We'll need that for his insurance, and for you to own the house."

"You'll be owner too, I think."

"Yeah?"

Lyle thought, but didn't say, that things were looking up. There'd be hassle and expense for Dad's funeral, but it could be paid out of the insurance and he and Faith would be in good shape. He was feeling calmly satisfied, Faith relaxing also in response to the wine, when a couple of vehicles crunched the gravel outside. Their lights were bright but not flashing, their sirens had not sounded.

Lyle sat in near-darkness at the kitchen table, a cup of instant coffee at hand. It was between three and four in the morning. At what point, he wondered, had the uniformed cops seen fit to call in the detective? Maybe it was all the liquor in the living room and on their breaths, some anomaly in the bedroom, or their delay in calling anyone after the discovery. Possibly the funeral director had implied some suspicion when he notified them. The detective was clearly skeptical, especially toward Faith, eyeing Lyle as he might a dense or deluded drunk. They'd be getting interviewed again at the police station, probably after the autopsy on Dad. The neighbors had watched him taken away, no doubt. Ben would be around at first light wanting all the details, giving the customary offer of help. Lyle felt lacking in details himself, though as always he could use the help.

He got up and stretched, then started in quietly on the kitchen drawers and cabinets. Where were those two prescription bottles? He felt an encroaching need to find them, maybe get rid of them. Faith could be in some trouble. He absolutely could not afford to lose her, had to prevent it. He wouldn't tell her that he'd read the thoughts of the police, that he saw a pattern for events developing, a grave danger. He'd just secretly protect her so things would stay the same between them.

He went through the living room next, then the bathroom. The effort to stay silent made him nervous. He failed to locate the containers.

"What were you doing?" Faith asked as he got back in bed.

"Nothing. Just moping around. Couldn't sleep."

Ben was watching from his kitchen window as the police returned in late morning and showed Faith and Lyle a search warrant. The searchers spread out through the house and outside, inspecting everywhere, while the couple stood abjectly on their sidewalk. Ben did his neighborly duty, exiting his house and brimming with righteous concern as he approached the couple. The day was cool and breezy with a mostly cloudy sky.

"Dad passed away last night," Faith explained.

"I saw them take him away," Ben said. "My deepest sympathy." He gave a sincere bow. "But what are they doing back here? Why don't they leave you in peace?"

"It seems like they're suspicious of us," Faith answered, "about how Dad died. Or maybe just of me. I was sitting with him when he went."

"We were a little late making the call," said Lyle. "The shock, wondering what to do."

"Sure," Ben commiserated, "I can see that."

He watched with them briefly as the searching went on.

"Like to come over for coffee till they finish here? Get out of the wind?"

"Can't," said Faith. "They told us to stick around."

She looked over at a policeman who'd stayed with the cars.

"Oh. Well, let me know if I can be of any help."

Ben returned over the gravel to his own property. From the shack next to the place being searched a tall man emerged with a basket of wet laundry.

"Christ," muttered Lyle, "does he have to do that now?"

Faith shrugged.

"In his mind, yes, he has to. This is where we are now, Lyle. This place, these people. It's our present destiny in the universe."

"Thanks for putting me right," he said.

But he wondered if she'd shown dissatisfaction. Something he'd maybe fed into. His complacency, his emotional dependence on her. She'd been great with her patience toward him, but then with her caring for Dad and all--well, things added up and people had their limits, even Faith. This physical location, their circumstances, their getting older, the sense of descending on the social scale. She might've felt pushed to do something drastic, even at the expense of her principles. The once unimaginable became the necessary.

The police search proved to be fruitless, as Lyle's had been, but the autopsy findings that prompted it also required forensic toxicology analysis. Samples for the laboratory were taken from Dad's body and it was released to the funeral home. A provisional death certificate was issued, the cause of death listed as "pending investigation."

He might have imagined it, Lyle thought, but a thick cloud of suspicion seemed to hang over him and Faith during the funeral and luncheon. They sat together meekly, he hoping their reticence would be attributed to grief. But a wildfire of gossip could have been raging among the relatives. An innocuous couple was emerging as culpable--more of their present destiny--but partly again the result of his early decisions in life. Whatever Faith had done to cause their situation, he himself would not be in it if he'd followed the correct- -the logical--course in his choice of work and relationships. Instead of developing into a revered member of the literati, he'd chosen to be a pretentious bureaucrat, sanctimoniously dumping taxpayer dollars into a whirlpool of waste. His direction in life was set, his attempts later to change it taking him further into the swamp.

Eleven days after the police search of their home, the detective they'd met returned with two patrol cops--one a woman--and a warrant for Faith's arrest. Ben watched from across the gravel as she was led down their front steps in handcuffs and placed in a patrol car. He waited anxiously for the group to leave and then hastened over to see Lyle.

"Third-degree manslaughter," the husband informed him.

"What! But there's no evidence, is there?"

"Circumstantial. The toxicology report showed an overdose of fentanyl in his system. His pain killer. Also a ton of loprazolam, something to help sleeping."

"So how do they pin it on Faith?"

"Mostly the long time she was with him while he died. Not calling the responders. If they could've found more evidence, like the drug bottles with too much gone, she might be up for murder."

Ben took a moment to absorb this.

"So what will you do?" he asked.

"See about a lawyer, I guess. Try to support her, see her when I can."

Ben withdrew to let Lyle make his arrangements. He could well sympathize with a man left alone in a house. He himself was missing Patty, his beautiful daughter, who was gone for an extended time in her stewardess role. He had only his paying boarders, who lived upstairs and had their own entrance. But Patty would return soon, Ben knew, so he was far better off than his secluded neighbor across the way.

Ben did not yet realize that, while taking the sun before leaving for the airport, Patty had noticed something strange in the distance. Through sunglasses and glare she'd seen a hand and wrist protrude from Dad's window and fling two small objects over the tall cyclone fence bordering the nuns' field. The items were lost to sight in the mass of tall weeds.

She could not have identified the age, race, or gender of the thrower.

THE DEMOTIONS

People stood around the file bins in the middle of the module, everyone applauding except me and Kenneth, he finally giving a few desultory claps. A promotion had been announced, one we'd expected to be mine. I'd been rated high for five and one-half years, had mentored new workers, and had twice filled the promotion position temporarily. The person being applauded could not match these qualifications. But affirmative action was in effect, asserting the overriding factors of gender and ethnicity.

"I don't know what to tell you," Ken said back at our desks. "Maybe you could make yourself more noticeable somehow. Controversial. Less majority-like."

He was a few years older than me, held a slightly higher position. He'd started at a time of less challenge to one's identity.

"No," I said to him. "I don't think so."

"Yeah? Well, you never know."

"True enough. But I've been through this before."

This was in December, 1983, reflection during the holiday season to follow.

———————

Seven and one-half years previous, I sat in a small room with an administrator and her assistant, door closed. It was a 24-hour operation, I supervising the day shift. My position, along with those of the evening and midnight shift supervisors, was to be upgraded with a new title and raise in pay. But I was not to retain the position.

"We'll be filling it with an outside applicant," said the administrator. "You'll be her assistant, keeping your present job title and pay grade."

"So, how do you feel about this?" asked the assistant, a slim aging woman with neat hairdo.

"Well," I answered with restraint, "of course I'm disappointed. I'd assumed I'd be promoted like the others, having more people to supervise and more activity on the shift."

"Yes," said the administrator, "but you've also had administrative staff here during the day, backing you up."

"You're very young to be in management," blurted the assistant. There will be other opportunities for you."

"Actually," the administrator added hastily, "you were in contention right up to our decision date. It was a late application, a surprise really, but her qualifications are excellent. She'll be a great help to the program."

I sat silently, they awaiting my reaction. I hedged, mentioning my relationship with the workers, how it would change with the new manager, likely difficulties for myself and others. They were slow to respond so I said maybe I should just move on.

"But," said the assistant, "where will you go? Leaving us all of a sudden like that?"

I gave a slight shrug, a forced smile.

"I'll be all right."

"There's another possibility," said the administrator.

It sounded rehearsed as she described it--an opening in a satellite unit under her authority, housed in a building under someone else. The office was closer to my apartment, to which I'd moved just recently. The work involved much less pressure.

"Can I let you know tomorrow?" I asked.

"Sure. Shall we say nine a.m.?"

"Okay."

Three-fourths of a decade later, I returned to the same duties I'd had before another non-promotion, this time without a sweetener. The memos, the paperwork, the office talk and routines all took on a bitter flavor, a suffocating stagnancy that seemed to mock my efforts and the new fatigue I felt, a downward spiral toward purposelessness. Even my trainee, a pleasant young woman whom I'd enjoyed mentoring, became a burden. I'd not been treated fairly so I lived and worked with anger. It was worse this time because I'd acquired a family, was approaching middle age. My accuracy and output slipped, attracting the notice of an obnoxious assistant manager.

"Why are all those records piled in your leg space?" Ken asked.

"That's my trainee's work. Wandine said to not review anything till I'm caught up with my own stuff."

He gave a puzzled look.

"They're all gonna be on the late list. She's technically not your supervisor, right? Maybe you should talk with the others."

"No, I think I'll let the chips fall. Let her answer for it."

He reflected a moment, nodded noncommittally.

"Good luck."

———\\\\———

My compliance with the transfer years before had seemed a decent move at first. The people in my unit were pleasant enough to work with, the supervisor especially so. I was her assistant, supervising as needed in her absence, no superior present since we weren't under the site administrator. We were more or less outsiders to others in the office, but I found the situation quite comfortable. I'd forgotten a remark our administrator had made in granting the transfer.

"It will give you some time, anyway."

I'd briefly understood she meant time to do a search and obtain other employment, a suitable career move. This came home to me after a few months in my niche when she announced that the satellite units were to be centralized. We were to be moved, along with several other groups, to the very building I'd left in humiliation. This was revealed at a meeting for supervisors, one I attended for my supervisor who was off. Though I was well down the table, the administrator eyed me specifically when she invited questions.

"Anything you want to ask, Don?"

"Ah, no. I'll pass the info along."

"Good."

———※———

As 1984 dragged on, winter into spring, there were increasing conflicts with Wandine. So many cases on the late list, both the trainee's and my own, increasing errors, and her oft-spoken observation that I sat staring into space. Ken was amused by her sniping and I pretended the same. But within me festered a growing resentment, countermanding any orders I received in proportion to the force with which they were given. As an employee, even to other management, I must have appeared uncaring and out of control. I eventually wound up in a small room with Borch, my evaluating supervisor with whom I'd had little contact.

"I haven't been in the module long," he said, "nor has our manager, so we have to respect Wandine's input on operations."

I waited silently, glad for the break in routine.

"Of course," Borch continued, "there are statistics."

He held up some sheets with both hands.

"There seem to be some problems with your performance."

"What sort of problems?"

He resorted to the sheets, began with some technobabble, then flipped the papers aside.

"I think you're aware of all this. What it amounts to is, we want you to come back on board. We're relieving you of your mentoring duties. Just concentrate on your own work, get those stats back up, and we'll see how you're doing in a month or so."

"All right," I nodded.

"Would you like a referral to Employee Counseling?"

"Why would I want that?"

"I'm required to ask."

The winter of 1976-77 was particularly harsh, making work out of my office of non-promotion even less pleasant than expected. I had added duties under the new setup, crowded work space, and many distant appointments through the heavy snows. I'd joked with a few people about quitting after New Year's, actually half serious, but a sort of inertia set in, a disingenuous optimism that enabled me to do nothing. I refused to deal with the fact that things couldn't--shouldn't--just go on. The nascent resentment within me was thus allowed to mature and take control. It would inevitably break through when the time, the setting, the circumstances could not contain it.

"You shouldn't have closed this case," said the newly-promoted assistant administrator. "Go get me the record."

She'd fielded a complaint in lieu of my vacationing supervisor. Given to snap judgments, this was a loud, heavy woman who favored multiple necklaces of large beads and wore many rings. Some called her The Bull. We'd worked at the same level when I was first hired.

"I believe a closed case is supposed to go through Intake if a new report is received."

"This isn't a new report. It's the old report you shouldn't have closed out."

"My supervisor signed off on it. It's closed within the system."

"I don't care. Get the record so I can read it."

I got up and left her stuffy little room. I walked toward the secretarial pool where the closed file cabinets stood along a wall. Once there, however, I walked straight through, made another turn, and returned to my own office. Donning my coat and grabbing my briefcase, I took leave of my colleagues and left the building.

Yes, I reflected after talking with Borch, just like with The Bull I could not be Wandine's go-fer. That was what getting "back on board" would mean. The month of trial passed and, though I missed talking with my former trainee, I continued to work without deference to my harasser's nagging. She sometimes lost control, criticizing me loudly across the module while puffing on her cigarillo. This particular smoking habit of hers became emblematic for me of her negative attributes, she a modified version of the stereotypic cigar-chomping boss. I didn't see why her opinion of me should be taken all that seriously. Yet there I was back in the tiny room with Borch, he reporting in sorrowful tones that I had not sufficiently progressed and so managerial action was necessary. The best he could do for me was a demotion to three pay grades below, the level at which I'd started six years before.

"You would be in a different module," he added. "You could work your way up again, of course."

"And there's no alternative?"

"No, I'm afraid not. Nothing better, I mean, on our end."

"Other than me resigning."

"That's up to you."

———※———

It had also been up to me the other time, of course. But I'd chosen to stay, had that incident with The Bull, then served a week's suspension as she vindictively followed through. My true supervisor chose to quit, her work relationships spoiled. Our unit was placed under a bushy-bearded lunatic who'd been dead weight in operations. He showed his gratitude by micromanaging myself and a close colleague, eventually recommending me for firing. The administrator seemed insecure at my disciplinary hearing, surrounding herself with her assistants and all her supervisors, now conveniently in the building due to centralization. The sight of them as the bush-beard blathered engendered nausea within me.

"I've had enough," I told my representative during a break. "I'd like you to tell them I'll resign."

"Are you sure? There's plenty we can fight them with."

"No. It's overdue for me. By a year at least."

The latest conference with Borch had left me confused. Faced again with a choice between resignation and humiliation, I was loath to accept the latter after my experience of years past. To willingly enter a reduced state or lesser role was to step into a downward spiral, an accelerating descent to spiritual ruin. And yet I couldn't just walk away. I had a family now and was significantly older. Perhaps I'd been wrong or excessive in my reaction to the non-promotion, but much of it was involuntary, a seething indignation arising from primal instincts. The stage had been set in my earlier job and remained in place until now.

"They want an answer by three p.m. Friday," I said to Ken.

He gave a start, looking up from his policy and procedure manuals.

"You got something else lined up?"

"No."

"That's a bitch. Not much choice then, is there?"

I looked away from him, scanned the open floor plan containing the modules, the file cabinets and clerks in the middle, the privacy screens around managers' desks.

"Anybody ever bring a gun in here?"

He hesitated.

"Whoa there, now. Hold on. How about drinks after work? Kick it around *then*."

"Okay."

But our discussion at the train station bar didn't resolve anything. Ken steered my mention of guns toward conversation on hunting, then sports in general, then somehow onto women, at the office and elsewhere. Wandine was not mentioned. By the time we'd finished drinking and parted for our respective trains, we were no longer mindful of my crisis. It returned to me later, of course, and I searched at home for my gun owner's permit, never used to purchase but still valid. I recalled a .32 caliber revolver I'd considered buying once, holding it in a sporting goods store, liking the feel and moderate weight. There was a three-day waiting period, however, and I didn't follow through. I now saw that the requirement precluded arming myself before the Friday deadline.

Wandine would have been a logical target if I'd gone the gun route, along with some others. I watched her moving about as I tried to form another plan. Quitting was out of the question, though maybe not if accompanied by a sufficient parting shot, a salvo of resentment toward the corruption that impeded me. Something that wasn't self-destructive, I now saw, yet stronger than just a spoken or written statement. There were tendencies in life that were working against me and had to be diverted. I needed to serve notice to the demons.

But Wednesday passed, then Thursday. The well of inspiration had run dry for me. I'd had only fleeting notions that were of no use in making a plan.

On Friday, I sat at my desk not working, closely watching Wandine as she went about the module, occasionally disappearing into the file cabinets or elsewhere. On one such foray, she strode a far distance toward the office of the section chief, boss over six modules. My gaze drifted back to Wandine's desk in a windowed corner of the floor. I had a good view of it between her privacy screens and noticed that she'd left her cigarillo smoldering on the edge of an aluminum ashtray. Something awoke in my mind, an idea first hazy but slowly gaining clarity. I picked up a folder from my desk and slipped along the wall behind me toward Wandine's corner. Nobody paid me any heed. I could have been simply delivering some work to her.

My thoughts raced as I stood behind her desk, which was cluttered with documents, bulletins, newspapers, receipts, Kleenexes, Styrofoam, and paper cups. All flammable. With a single smooth movement I could bridge the mess to the burning cigarillo. A narrow bridge, allowing me time to return calmly to my desk, retaining the folder I'd brought. I savored the thought of Wandine being held responsible for the outcome. I maneuvered into better position, glancing up to ensure no one was watching.

But as my hand moved forward to shift a couple of policy bulletins, I had a vision of the possible calamity. There might be chaos and many injuries, and I might somehow be found out, face disgrace and prison. My family would suffer also. I couldn't live with all that. Not with any of it.

My hand changed course, reached for and grabbed the cigarillo itself, stubbed it out hard against the ashtray. The extinguished end was so flattened and widened the cigarillo could stand on end.

Back at my desk, I opened the folder I'd been carrying and spread the contents before me. A prop. I sat with my hands on my thighs, drumming my fingers occasionally, looking into the middle distance. My mind was a blank, resigned and waiting. Ken eventually noticed.

"You gonna talk with them, Don? Cutting it mighty close."

"Yeah, well. I think I'll let them *come to me*."

He started to smile.

"Play chicken with them? I don't know. Most people would act while they still had options."

"I'm not most people. And I'm done with their options."

Ken shrugged and edged back toward his manuals.

"Okay, tiger. I'm buying later."

I resumed my stance, staring into space. Borch appeared promptly at three o'clock, coming down the aisle with an envelope and moving carton, security guard in tow. Wandine stood at a distance next to the module manager, neither woman smoking. Farther off, poking up above the file cabinets, I saw the head of the section chief. It appeared he was watching through binoculars.

EXECUTIONER

The work at the office supply store had grown tedious and Wayne had always thought it beneath him, so he was watchful for something better, an enhancement. He felt a need for significance, respect, perhaps even uniqueness. He was short on education and possessed no particular skill, so the professional world was out. There were training programs but he was inherently undisciplined. He could assist customers who came into the store, help one find a product or work a copier or fax machine, but he was not a people person. He preferred to work silently and alone.

Yet he wanted to feel ennobled. Iconic, even.

In the news people were gaining brief fame by doing dumb stunts. This was not for Wayne, however, since the distinction he desired would be ongoing, no end in sight, and remunerative. He was well aware that he had little to offer and was also rather lazy. But somewhere, he thought, there existed his niche. It could be something most people wouldn't want, since he'd then face little competition. This suggested danger or something disgusting. Danger was out for him, of course, so what work would be disgusting but distinctive? Nothing involving substances for Wayne, but what about offensiveness to feel-good values? He recalled a news snippet about the shortage of people willing to administer capital punishment. A photo had shown a man in black hood about to throw a large electrical switch. He was dumpily built and wore an everyday shirt with large black and white checks. He stood in an isolated position behind the prisoner in the chair being prepared by officials.

I could do that, Wayne thought, and I wouldn't be wearing a dumb shirt and slouching like a mope.

There was power in the position, he considered later. The ender of life, not as a common criminal, the scum of the earth, but as a sanctioned agent of legitimate government authority. He would free the planet from the toxic presence of vicious and incorrigible creatures who'd forfeited their existence by committing horrible crimes. They were, in a sense, their own executioners, but they did not deserve the honor. That would be his own.

He called the state personnel office, told a drowsy-sounding woman he was looking for corrections work, mentioned the executioner shortage.

"Are you eighteen or over?"

"Yes."

"High school graduate?"

"Yes."

"You can print out the application form from our website. For the position number write 0316X. Title: Auxiliary Corrections Technician I (Part Time). Send it to the address on the form but add 'Attention Mr. Holgate.'"

"Is that two *L*s or one?"

"Just one."

Wayne got right to it. It occurred to him, though, that "part time" might well mean "as needed," and there weren't a lot of executions in the news. Perhaps he should try applying in neighboring states as well to increase his prospects for action. They would normally favor their own citizens for state work but this was a shortage situation. The liberal states to the west and north had abolished capital punishment, but to the east and south were three nearby states which might welcome his services. He therefore bore down and was soon sending letters and forms to these states as well.

He kept his project secret from coworkers at the office supply store. He knew the activity he wished to enter was a sensitive subject to some, a potential threat to camaraderie and even his employment itself. Likewise, he resolved to not tell his relatives whom he rarely saw anyway. There was, however, a young woman in the building who'd often crossed his path and become a friendly acquaintance. They'd shared a couple of walks and agreed to meet for lunch or something at an indefinite date. She was rather plain, short and limp-haired, but pleasingly unobtrusive. Wayne felt a need to have someone else know his plan and thought Jana would do.

"But why do you want to do this?" she asked.

They were having ice cream at an outdoor table of a casual neighborhood coffee shop. It was the cool evening of a very warm day.

"To have something more," Wayne replied. "An addition to the ordinary life. Something of importance."

"Aren't there other things of importance that you might find, well, more pleasant?"

"The thing is, I believe in this."

"Oh. Well, one must do what one believes in."

We both took tastes of ice cream.

"I was wondering," Wayne said. "What sort of place would you like if we went out to dinner?"

A delicate, fragile smile crossed Jana's lips.

"Do you mind Czech food?"

She helped to pass the interlude as he awaited responses to his inquiries. There had been mentions in the postings of experience with chemicals or electric circuits being desirable but not necessary. Again, he relied on the shortage of applicants to obviate such qualifications. He had every confidence in his project, was resolved and looked forward to following through, and so was calmly satisfied when the first opportunity arrived. It was in the southernmost state of his group, the farthest he could reasonably drive to. He'd have to pay for a motel but considered the expense worthwhile.

On the day preceding the execution he called in sick to work and drove southward along unfamiliar highways. The tedium of the drive allowed flickers of doubt to nag him, the crossings of state lines his only evidence of progress. The surrounding landscape grew increasingly dull, oppressive, a venue for rural futility. The sky clouded over. When he finally reached his motel he felt exhausted, not only physically but somehow mentally. He must shake it off, he told himself, regain his drive, the sense of purpose that was new and vital to him. He accordingly showered and lay down to rest before dinner, but then woke in the middle of the night with no source of food except a lobby vending machine.

Wayne stayed up the rest of the night with nothing to do. He kept watch on the nearest fast-food restaurant, indulging gluttonously as soon as it opened.

Arriving at the prison, he was escorted to a small room and given a form to complete and sign. Two other men were at the table where they all sat in cheap plastic chairs. One man was tall with unkempt red hair and longish beard, the other dark complexioned and thickly built. The red-haired man was still puzzling over his form, the dark man sitting with arms folded and completed form before him.

"Where y'all from?" the tall man asked.

Wayne told him.

"Long way from home."

Wayne said nothing.

"Done this before?"

"No."

"Rookie. Got a couple under my belt. Nothin' to it. Lot easier'n wit' hogs." Then, to the other man: "How 'bout you?"

"Got you beat by plenty."

Wayne focused on the form, especially the address to which payment should be sent. He didn't know how much it would be but thought it must be a good amount for the others to be there. He hadn't foreseen having company in his role, though he'd known there'd be others observing and guarding. He could just play things by ear, he thought, till it was time to deal the death blow. Then his right move would be obvious. Easy, just like Red Beard had said.

A guard came in and collected the forms, led them from the room and through a series of hallways, down a staircase on the way, stopping outside a room in which they could see a fragile apparatus being checked. It was an upright frame holding three large syringes inserted into IV tubes leading through a curtained window to the front. When the technicians were satisfied, Wayne and his companions were furnished masks and allowed into the room. A suited official gave instructions on when each of them should push the plunger on his syringe. Signals were to be given by the official in front of the window, on which the curtain would be opened. The suited man left and soon, too soon for Wayne, the curtain flew open and the room for death was displayed. A man had been strapped to a gurney, IVs in both arms, with several attendants standing around him. There were ten or so observers in folding chairs down the room. They were still as statues.

Wayne stood at the middle syringe watching final preparations: inspection of the connections and valves on IVs, the prisoner shaking his head *no* when questioned by an official. Three guards came into the executioners' room and took up positions behind Wayne and the others.

"In case someone don't function," muttered Red Beard.

"Why don't they do this to start with?"

"Cause they got us," said the dark man.

Wayne began to feel out of sync, as if he didn't belong in the situation. It could be lack of sleep, he thought, the huge breakfast, or the long drive and geographic shift. But he wasn't totally out of it, he told himself. He could and would follow through on this. He had to. He was committed to it.

There eventually came a pause when everyone was still. The official in charge raised his hand beyond the window, then raised the index finger. Red Beard, to Wayne's left, immediately depressed his plunger, emitting a slight gasp at the finish. An excruciating interval followed for Wayne, during which he envisioned hellfire, Moses haranguing a mob, the stormy sky over Calvary. But two fingers were being raised. A second, maybe two, of hesitation by Wayne, then the plunger was being pressed and by his hand, ending for the moment his own pain, the horrible conflict. It was done, finished for him. He remained staring at the syringe while the man on his right completed the execution.

The rest was a blur to him: vague memories of a different, shorter route out of the prison, a guard watching them in the parking lot, odd looks from Red Beard, a cynical remark from the other man. He left the lot as required but parked a short distance away. He felt stunned, his brain was numb, he couldn't think. He knew he had the long drive home but something was wrong with that. He wasn't in condition for it, that must be the thing, it wouldn't be safe. He drove to his motel from the night before and arranged to stay there again. Within a minute of entering his room he collapsed onto the bed and slept until late afternoon. On waking, he called out for pizza and decided to also call Jana.

"How did it go?" she asked.

"Oh, I'll tell you about it later. I just called to, ah, to talk with someone. To hear your voice."

"Are you all right?"

"Sure, I'm okay. A little drained is all. I'm staying over again tonight and then I'll drive back tomorrow."

"Good. Let me know when you're here. Any time's okay."

"I'll do that. For sure."

"Fine. Well, drive safely as they say."

It wasn't much but the talk settled Wayne. He felt reassured, but in a different way now from before. He couldn't yet define it. He'd have to parcel out his feelings to Jana and get her reactions, draw on her for understanding. One thing, though, he already felt sure of: he was through as an executioner.

He took a shower and slept soundly despite the nap he'd taken.

———⋙———

Back in the day-to-day life he'd considered mundane, Wayne showed new energy and interest in his work and the people he dealt with. They, in turn, seemed to appreciate his change and to like and respect him more. He grew in self-confidence, not needing the false power he'd sought. But the reasons for all this he shared only with Jana. They saw much more of each other now, their restaurant outings becoming frequent. Jana was encouraging to Wayne, but with notes of caution, as if ever conscious of the fragility of happiness. She eventually told him of her policeman husband who'd been killed guarding a housing project.

"Terrible," Wayne responded.

"Yes. It's been some time now. We were very young."

"Was there, ah, prosecution?"

Jana nodded.

"Death sentence at first, commuted by a later governor."

Wayne didn't know what to say.

"So then you moved here."

"Yes, I couldn't stand it there. I needed change."

"I'm glad you picked here."

The subjects of capital punishment and Wayne's participation in it were tacitly abandoned in their conversations. At the office supply store, however, less busy work days invited discussion of current news stories, including volatile issues. Horrific crimes continued to dominate headlines, especially during any lull in warfare or disease proliferation. The prevailing opinion was for maximum punishment of any perpetrators. Wayne expressed mild agreement to get along on the job, inwardly restrained by thoughts of his recent experience, and of Jana. A part of him had changed, he thought, but a part of him had not. Support for his old attitude was encroaching on his newfound perspective.

"Maybe I was just weak," he said to Jana. "Like I didn't really make any decision, I just sort of caved inside. I went ahead and squeezed the syringe, fighting against it being wrong, just deciding that later to excuse my weakness. Like it wasn't right but I had to do it because of the others, and I was committed. So I wanted to do right but I was stuck. But that's all just an excuse. I was really just too weak, maybe, to go strongly one way or the other."

"You said you believed in it," she responded. "You saw some things and it changed your belief. That's all it is. Perfectly natural. You shouldn't beat yourself up over it."

"It's the details of the thing," Wayne thought aloud, "seeing and hearing--touching even--those details. So much different than people talking loud and know-it-all so far away from it."

"You think they're wrong now? The whole thing is wrong?"

He hesitated. That wasn't what he'd meant.

"No, not entirely. I'm not one to carry it out, I guess, but overall, well, I don't know--"

"All right, Wayne. Don't worry. It will all come clear in time. In the meantime we have us, each other, whatever madness there is out there."

He looked into her eyes.

"Yes. For that I'm grateful."

<hr/>

A letter arrived regarding another planned execution, this time in the state just east of Wayne's. Electrocution, chosen by a prisoner with extreme aversion to needles. The letter disturbed Wayne. He would have welcomed it before, seen it as opportunity made to order, but now it came as something he didn't want to deal with. Not that he could simply throw it away. He still respected the practice, wanted it to go ahead, but was apparently unable to be personally involved. Something held him back, deep in his psyche or his heart. He could only lay the letter aside and stew over it.

Later, in Jana's apartment, he told her about the letter.

"So, you're in demand," she said.

"Demand," he repeated thoughtfully, "yes."

"Think you'll be going?"

He was willing to feign an attitude to match her own, for the sake of their dialogue, relationship, but she was noncommittal.

"Actually," he said, "I'm on the fence about it."

She gave a little smile.

"Shaky up there."

"Yes."

"Stay here a minute, will you? There's something I've been meaning to show you."

She got up and left the room. There were crickets chirping beyond the open window and something that made a quack-like sound. It was a late summer evening. When Jana returned she was carrying a .38 caliber revolver.

"My late husband's," she explained.

"Is it loaded?"

"No, but I have the bullets for it."

"A house gun, but for intruders it should be loaded."

"That's not why I kept it."

"No?"

"No. It's to take care of his killer if he's released."

"It's a life sentence."

"They let them out anyway, the politicians."

"So you're thinking, then, execution?"

Jana nodded.

"But I'm on the fence about it," she said, "like you are. I can't go through with it because I'm prevented. Or maybe it's two different fences, not quite the same, and they intersect and we see each other, together with our separate conflicts. Different but somehow the same, the effects I mean if they're ever resolved."

Wayne hesitated, not quite following her, then reached out and gingerly took the gun.

"Easy, now. Relax. Just relax. We're here together. That's all that really counts."

He stayed with her as the hour grew late, then returned to his own apartment.

QUALITIES OF MERCY

We made our way through the last stretch of dry, aggressive weeds toward the cabin. Evening chill was already moving in under a billowing gray sky. Our take for the day's hunt was zero, Norm having taken our only shot, the animal obscured by leaves and barely within range.

"You don't think I winged it?" he asked as he brought out the brandy.

"Nah. I saw leaves kick up front left."

"Could've been wind."

"Right at that instant? Too much coincidence."

"Hope you're right."

I knew what he meant. The sin of leaving a wounded animal in the brush. We couldn't endure that as our day's result. We wanted to feel at peace as we sat with our drinks.

"It'd be evil, Jack."

"Yeah, but relax. It bolted full speed with the report."

We sipped and reflected, then Norm recalled our toast.

"To our friends and enemies!"

"Can't have one without the other!"

Our usual low chuckling, then again the low clouds.

"So much evil around, you know?"

I gave a grunt and a nod.

"Guess it's always been that way," he continued. "Some say Satan rules the earth, but I don't quite believe it. More like an uneasy truce. But he's often got the upper hand. Lack of scruples, you know? No morality holding him back, that extra edge for the aggressor."

"Still a violent world, all right. Civilization under siege."

Norm stared into the middle distance.

"My grandfathers were both violent men. My father too, of course. His earliest memory was being slapped to the floor as a three-year-old. His oldest picture had him in a ballerina dress. Said women then liked to dress little boys that way. Maybe some connection to the slapping."

"So, a legacy of abuse, so to speak."

"Ah, something more general. His father was a cop and they were a lot rougher then. Made today's guys look like missionaries. He fathered thirteen kids and then left the home. There were lots of issues."

"And your other grandfather?"

"Also that seed of violence, but in his case directed inward. Hung himself from a tree by the public library. Two small children left behind, a widow left to cope, her younger sister coming in as second parent, never herself getting married."

I wasn't inclined like Norm to discuss my family, even as the brandy flowed. So as he described his father's slapping and belt attacks, his mother's collaboration, I plucked from my past an abusive teacher to divert the conversation. A second-year Latin instructor, this religious brother was known to his students as Publius, a character from our first-year text. He wielded in his class a yard-long dowel from the shop classes, which he called a "doll rod" in his Alabama accent. It was freely applied to backsides for breaches of silence or anything else that irritated him, including imperfect translations. The victim was required to bend forward with his hands on a middle front desk, facing the class, his humiliation thus maximized as Publius swung with all his might. The punisher was a short and scrawny man who appeared to relish this exercise of power. For the first grading period he gave *F*s to 22 out of forty in our class.

"What did he give you?" Norm asked.

"I got a *C*. But he never tired of calling me lazy, and I got my share of the doll rod."

"Glad I went to the public school. Ran into some of that later,

70

though, when I first started working. There was this one guy, one of the butchers at the supermarket. Used to come up behind me and get me in a bear hug, hard, lift me off the ground that way. He'd hold it a long time then drop me with some insult. Gave me grief whenever he could. Finally told the manager I was a lousy worker so they let me go."

"You didn't get to tell your side?"

"I wasn't in the union yet. Moron timed it so he'd bug me till I was almost eligible, then get rid of me."

"Gratuitous hatred."

"Crops up everywhere. I saw it again at the cookie factory, then the printing plant. A little bit of authority opening the gates to aggression. Old pent-up anger and biases finding vulnerable targets, people just objects for someone's gratification."

"Something like a rape mentality."

"Yeah. Sounds extreme but in that direction. Good point, Jack."

"Actually, I found myself in the middle of it at a place I worked."

"You mean, you were--"

"No, not a victim. An unknowing acquaintance. There were two of them as it turned out. One of them sat behind me. Tall, husky guy, premature balding. Talked in a deep, rumbling voice, had a glowering expression. Short of temper. Despite all that, we were shocked when he was arrested for luring a fifteen-year-old girl into his van. All of us, that is, except the man sitting next to me. We'd worked in the same unit since I'd started, got along great. We were friends outside of work, I'd met his wife. Both attractive people. He'd been a college football player and played in a major bowl game. I used to wonder why he didn't have a better job. Then, after I was promoted out of the office, I found he'd been indicted in college for raping a college stenographer. The court case was pending back in the college town the whole time I knew him."

Norm stared at me, eyebrows raised, set down his glass and got up.

"Need a smoke," he said, and headed for the cabin door.

He'd taken one cigarette and left the pack on the table. Time was when I'd have joined him, but my habits had moderated more than his. Instead I drifted to one of the cabin windows and peered into the engulfing gloom. I wasn't entirely sure, actually, about the animal escaping unhurt. I'd simply wanted to settle Norm's doubts, gain needed resolution in our short lifetimes of constant moral ambivalence. The story of Publius had been truncated as well. I could have added that, following the academic year, we'd seen each other in a restaurant where I was working for the summer. He was staring at me from a distance where he sat a table with a woman about his age. He was in sporty clothes, not his black religious garb and collar, and she appeared rather giddy. I was serving up desserts, including a couple that had gone to their table. I was told by the waitress later that his had gone uneaten. Also that he'd seemed irritated. The following school year he never once spoke to me, even though he'd become moderator of the debate team, which I was on. I found myself oddly demoted to the junior varsity, of which a different brother was in charge.

We should eat soon, I thought, and moved to get the cheese and French bread I'd picked up earlier. There were also apricots and chocolate, but I wasn't sure Norm would want them.

"That last story you told," he said back at the table, "about the guy under indictment, it brings to mind something else. More a situation than a person, but his name was Tom Goode. The name seemed to fit when you first saw him--clean faced, hair combed back, physically fit, alert, polite, married to a nice, friendly wife. Yet he'd been in prison for rape, convicted after a lengthy trial. It started with a bunch of accusers but then all but one were outwitted by his lawyers. Tom wound up going to prison for two years."

"You say he was married?"

"Yeah, to a counselor from the prison. Big horsey girl, tousled red hair. She helped get him out."

"You knew him before he went in?"

"No. First met him when a friend of mine from college had a group of old high school buddies over. Tom was recently released and they were edgy about his coming, but they relaxed once the drinks and conversation got going. Nobody mentioned the rapes or prison. The horsey girl seemed to help. A professional, of course."

"And they appeared, well, a normal couple?"

"Yeah, pretty much. I mean, they would if you didn't know about before. As it was, I think anyone who did know would be leery about having Tom around. It's not like he was cured of a physical illness."

"No, it's not so visible, and it's deep-seeded. No one knows when the violence will erupt again. I once had to interview a woman who'd been in prison for stabbing someone."

"Bet you were rather uneasy."

"There was another woman with her. Big, a stabilizing influence. The task got done and I was out of there."

"Always the best way. Finish up and show them your dust."

"Yes, when you can. But sometimes it can get tricky. Like when you can't just leave, you have responsibility. You have to deal with them."

Norm looked at me quizzically. The brandy was getting low, so he divided what was left between our glasses.

"We're still talking about violence?"

"Right."

I told him about Joan Prism, a worker I'd supervised. She was petite and pale with light blue eyes and thick flaxen hair. She'd started with several others when the group under me suddenly ballooned. At first she'd seemed just a little outspoken, otherwise rather mousey. I tried to hide the attraction I felt with her but she must have picked up on it. She grew more confident in her manner and one day burst into our director's office to give her take on some issue. He'd been in conference with his assistant, a cold and ambitious fellow who was angered by the intrusion. He ordered me to reprimand her with a written warning notice to be copied into her personnel file. Joan was livid when I did so, screaming and using profanity. Her mouth opened widely such that strings of saliva stretched between top and bottom. I'd closed the door to my small office for privacy but a couple of secretaries opened it in alarm. I shooed them away and tried to placate my out-of-control worker, saying whatever came to mind that was conciliatory.

After work, I'd hardly arrived at my apartment when I received a call from Joan saying she wanted to meet with me for drinks. I didn't recall exactly how we'd left things so I consented, assuming we were to finish discussing our problem like rational adults. There were several pubs and restaurants in my neighborhood that were decent settings for our talk. When she arrived at my building, however, she voiced concern about privacy and noise and suggested I make drinks for us in my apartment. Led by my still-present attraction to her, I agreed.

We sat on opposite ends of my couch, sipping our strong drinks, while she worked up to her subject. She was trying to stay calm. She said she'd wanted to kill me that afternoon, was glad nothing sharp had been handy, realized now that the administrators were her enemies. She grew suddenly tense as she said this, took a gulp of her drink, clenched her free hand. She glared into the middle distance and released a stream of invective about the assistant director. I let her vent, soon had to refresh our drinks. When she'd calmed a bit I suggested a plan: that she file a grievance about the warning notice and I would back her up with her union rep. After a moment she said she liked the idea, wanted to do it, and then she got pretty friendly. As friendly as she'd been hateful just a little while earlier.

Norm waited for more, but I'd gone as far as I intended.

"That's some story, Jack. A full reversal."

"Well, I still had to be careful with her. Like we said before, that capacity for violence, cruelty, sadism is deep-seated, still a threat no matter what's covering it up."

"Manners, social status and such."

"Right. Even education, professionalism. I heard a social worker once, soft-spoken girl from Louisiana, say that welfare mothers should all be sterilized."

"Fixed like with dogs."

"Yeah."

Norm shook his head, then appeared thoughtful.

"That reminds me of someone, fake minister I lived near. Went by 'El Cubano.' Held weird services in the backyard of his building. Put up a tent sometimes. Neighbor saw a goat led in from a van in the alley, did some spying. Turned out they were into animal sacrifice. The 'minister' took off before the cops could nab him. Nobody knew where he went, except probably to hell."

"Were you the neighbor?"

"Nah."

But Norm had stayed reflective, then frowned into deeper thought, his gaze drifting to our rifles in the corner. In a moment he was up. He donned his coat and grabbed a rifle by the barrel, then was rummaging through a drawer near the sink.

"Where's the flashlight?"

"Top of the fridge."

I didn't need to ask where he was going. I wanted to again assure him the animal was dead but I knew it wouldn't stop him.

"It's completely dark," I said, "even darker in the brush. Let it go, Norm. We can look around in the morning."

"Won't work, Jack. Not good enough."

He was quickly out of the cabin. I stepped outside myself and watched him charging off in the direction from which we'd arrived. He was silhouetted against the light beam sweeping before him, but that soon faded and Norm along with it. I listened for the faint sound of his tromping but that was gone too. Maybe, I thought, I should have finished the story of Ms. Prism. Told him of her clothes draped over a chair with her shoes nearby, she herself with me in the dim green love-light over the Murphy bed. Told him of the sense of empowerment I'd felt in controlling the evil within her, feeling that I was drawing on it, sharing in it as much as I wished, she in an ecstasy of giving. I could have told Norm how I'd enjoyed it.

Maybe then he wouldn't be out there, I thought, stumbling in the dark with the night beasts--he now maybe the prey.

THE TOWER HOME

A few months after my father's death, I learned I'd inherited from him a remote property in a far northern state. The place was unknown to us members of his family. My brother, who'd administered the estate, received a tax bill from the distant rural county containing the property. Upon inquiring, he found my father had purchased it many years before, listing himself and me as co-owners on the deed, which contained a transfer-on-death clause. I'd therefore become sole owner of the place with all attendant responsibilities.

"There's a vintage building on the land," Jerry told me. "Looks heavily wooded on the satellite view."

"Useless, you think?"

"There are farms nearby, so it might be arable. You could tell on inspection, I think, maybe get an estimate on clearing. You need to file documents up there anyway."

"And pay the tax bill."

"Well, yeah."

My only plan initially was to sell the surprise acquisition. I wasn't optimistic about the market value, but assumed it would at least cover the taxes and any liens. Jerry supplied the documentation of our father's death and I made the long drive northward. I started along a route I'd taken several times before, once during September like this time. The summer vacationers had mostly departed, the nights were cool, the reflections of campfire pleasant against the dark woods nearby. This time would be different, of course. It was business. But a warm familiarity grew in me as I passed all the pastures and forests, the hazy, hilly horizon that cradled my destination. While puzzled by my father's ownership up here, as well as his sharing it with me, I felt grateful to him for necessitating this trip. The sudden dullness of early retirement tends to welcome such a diversion.

I arrived around dusk in the town nearest the property. I'd reserved a motel room for two nights, thinking this adequate time to accomplish my tasks. The motel was very quiet and the woman at the desk helpful. She had a county map on which we could pinpoint the exact location of my property. It was well removed from any main road, embedded among the gravel and dirt back roads that wound among the trees and streams. Farms were fewer now and smaller.

"I've a friend runs a bed-and-breakfast up there," the woman said. "Nearby your place. They'll be closing soon, though. We're open year-round."

She showed me on the map where her friend's place was located. It looked close enough to mine to be viewed from the "vintage structure" Jerry had mentioned. That could only be, however, if the trees weren't too thick.

"Are there trails through the woods there?" I asked.

"Not unless the bears made them."

I set out next morning after breakfast at the nearest diner. My drive was easy at first with the well-researched directions, but there were several turns onto increasingly primitive roads. The ultimate one was just a weedy pair of tire tracks that dead-ended at my aged edifice. It was three stories but narrow in relation to its height, built of stone with battlements along a flat roof. The walls were vertical rather than sloping inward. Windows were narrow, some boarded but others with glass intact, none left broken. The surrounding yard was a potpourri of weeds, some attaining tree height. Against the building was an out-of-control explosion of wildflowers that clearly had once been cultivated. There was a short break in the mass leading to a large door with chipping dark green paint. I picked my steps carefully as I approached it, wary of snakes and other such greeters.

The door wouldn't budge, whether locked or jammed I couldn't tell. Returning to my car for a lever, I renewed my efforts with vigor. Still no success. Leaving the door, I fought through the overgrowth checking the windows. All were locked or boarded until I reached one behind a thorny rose tangle. It opened easily. I clambered up over the high rough windowsill and dropped onto the floor inside. I was in a kitchen with dining area that occupied the entire level, sparsely furnished with a corner spiral staircase leading upward. Getting to my feet, I examined the vintage appliances and some stacks of newspapers and magazines on the rudimentary table. The more recent issues, going back two or three years, chiefly concerned sports, outdoor life, and vehicles. But underneath or tied in bundles were women's magazines, newsletters, and journals concerning art, science, and literature. These were dated far in the past, decades in many cases.

I tried a light switch but with no reaction. The place no doubt depended for power on the rusty generator I'd noticed in back, sheltered by a rickety shed. I decided to try the staircase.

Ascending the iron spiral, I came into a musty living room with tattered rugs and lumpy antique seating. The shelves of old display cabinets were empty of whatever treasures they had held. By contrast with all this, the paintings spaced tastefully on the walls were of relatively recent creation. They were mostly of rural landscapes and signed *Tilda* by the artist. Peering closely at one with human figures–a man, a woman, and a boy–I found the features, build, and posture of the man to be familiar. I decided it was a likeness of my father.

I lingered awhile before the painting, wondering about its inspiration. I'd have liked to sit down, but the couch and chairs were in their sad state, not offering comfort for reflection. I had no idea who Tilda was, nor the woman or boy in the picture, but the setting reflected that which surrounded me, harboring this tower-like structure that someone had called home. My father had purchased it, owned it as I now did, but was his connection stronger than mere ownership? I'd never really known him well, never had a son's trust and confidence in him. There were too many blank pages for me in his history.

I returned to the spiral staircase, ascended seeking answers. The third floor was the tower's bedroom, a bare double bed to one side and a covered roll-away to the other. There was a fixture on the ceiling that had apparently held a privacy curtain. An antique bureau stood near the double bed, its drawers containing musty women's clothing. A search among the garments revealed only some mouse damage in the bottom drawer. Crossing the room, I inspected the roll-away bedclothes, found a sheathed dagger under the flattened pillow.

I returned to the spiral stairs, viewed their extension to a trapdoor leading to the roof. It had no visible lock. On climbing a few steps and pushing upward, I met stiff resistance but eventually budged the thing, albeit through a shower of ancient dirt and leaves.

The roof afforded a panoramic view of the surrounding land. Forest and farms, roads, streams, and grazing animals all awaited the artist's rendition. A decrepit easel for this purpose was wedged on its side against the parapet, braced by a rusty box that I guessed contained paints. Forcing the box open, I found I was partly right, the old tubes dried solid, but there was also a small transistor radio with dead and corroded battery. The radio had been personalized on one edge in more permanent paint. The inscription read simply *Mom*. I was reminded of the painting down below, wondered again about my father's role here, then replaced all the items as I'd found them and stood to leave. Before descending, however, I studied the expanse of forest between my tower and the bed and breakfast mentioned at the motel. Though the B&B was my closest neighbor, a hike through the intervening flora looked to be quite a struggle. The driving route was much longer but would still be preferable if I cared to visit.

⁓

During the afternoon I drove to the recorder's office in the county seat. I filed an affidavit of survivorship along with my father's death certificate and a revised deed. It all went smoothly, there being no liens or other encumbrances on the property. Later I thought to call Jerry, wanting to give him an update but also to help fill an evening that felt empty at the motel.

"I'm thinking I'll stay a couple more days," I told my brother, "put the place in some order. A little cleanup, some minor repairs."

"It'll need more than that before listing, don't you think?"

"Oh yeah, of course. But there might be more to this than just physical property. There's the chance Dad had other involvement up here."

"What kind of involvement, Brian?"

I related my discovery of the painting, the inscription on the radio, the types and dates of the magazines, the dagger.

"Do you recall him ever mentioning a Tilda?" I asked.

"Let's see, well, there was a call some years back. When Mom was still living. She took it and gave the message to Dad, something about a 'former friend' who'd passed away. But he acted like he'd never heard of the person."

"Same name?"

"That or something like it. Of course, Mom might have misspoken."

"Or else Dad didn't want to let on."

"Yeah, that's also possible."

In the morning I extended my motel reservation, then hired a local locksmith to fix the tower's proper entrance. I drove out to the place with a growing sense of commitment to it. I was now sole owner, had full authority to make changes, felt obliged to render the place decent however ragged its past had been. I made use of a worn broom I found in the kitchen closet, sweeping the bottom two floors but postponing the mess higher up from the trapdoor opening. Outside, I inspected the generator and was surprised to find the fuel in it almost clear. A plastic bottle of stabilizer in the shed indicated someone had used it to extend the fuel's viability. I turned on the fuel valve, shifted the choke rod, and braced myself for a struggle with the pull cord, there being no ignition or engine switch. After several fruitless tugs I was about to try cleaning the spark plug or air filter when suddenly I got a sputter. The motor sprang noisily to life on my next pull, shattering the serene peace of the countryside.

For lunch I had sandwiches I'd brought from town and warm beer. There was water available from a hand pump over the kitchen sink but I wasn't sure of its drinkability. Best to just use it for washing awhile, I thought, let it clear. The locksmith had no such qualms, however, when he came that afternoon, lustily quenching his thirst from working on the stubborn door. He did a fine job and I was freed to secure the rear-window "entrance."

Before returning to town I examined the area around the outhouse, which was in good shape but set far back from the tower. It was therefore engulfed not only by weeds, but by larger, coarser brush that I especially wanted to clear. I was inspecting this tangle when something farther on caught my eye. It was a little ways into the woods, on the ground and light in color, highlighted by rays from the declining sun that penetrated leafy boughs. I decided to check it out, picked my way through vegetation to a tiny clearing about the size of a double bed. The light that had attracted me was from a pile of whitish rocks illumined for the moment by dying sunlight. The pile was at one end of the clearing, which I now noticed was unnaturally rectangular. The shape was enhanced by some depression along its edges, as if the ground had been dug up and then loosely replaced, causing it to settle and define the shape of the hole.

Tilda's grave, I guessed.

———※———

I ruminated that evening on whether I should report my discovery to the authorities, but decided there wasn't any rush. I was speculating, after all, and the apparent burial would have been years before. At the same time, I felt more drawn to the property with it having this new layer of meaning for me. Perhaps I should spend a night there, I thought, get to know it more intimately. I could spend the next day on more cleanup and then rest from my labors in the bedroom, judge the feasibility of moving there from the motel. I slept well that night with the thought of sleeping next on my own property.

I spent much of the next morning sprucing up the tower's bedroom and attacking the roof itself with a shovel from my car. Lunch went a little better, sandwiches again but with the beer cooled a bit by the low-powered refrigerator. I was hacking down tree-like weeds with an axe when a sheriff's car eased into the dead end of my access road. Two men in khaki emerged from the front seat while a middle-aged woman exited the back. They approached me through the weeds.

"Gene?" the older man greeted me. "You're Gene, right?"

"No, I'm Brian. Brian Finnegan."

He looked skeptical. I'd left my wallet with ID in the tower.

"That's not him," the woman volunteered. "He's not that tall. Or that dignified."

"You know this guy Gene, then?" the officer continued with me. "Squatter who comes and goes?"

"I'm afraid not. I've only been around here a few days. Inherited this place from my father who died recently."

"You can prove that?"

"I was just at the county recorder's office day before yesterday. The deed has been revised to show me sole owner."

He relaxed, took a long look at the tower and its surroundings.

"Looks like you've got some work ahead of you."

He explained they'd come by because a man had been assaulted the night before in the woods between my property and the B&B. The woman with them was the B&B's owner. The victim was a paying guest at her place who'd been walking in the woods when he was clubbed with a heavy tree limb by the squatter, who accused him of "trespassing" on his digs. This Gene had been angered on finding his rear-window entrance secured along with other changes.

"I'm sure we'll be picking him up soon," the officer said, "but in the meantime you'd best not be around here much. You got a weapon?"

"Just this," I said holding the axe.

"Yeah, well. You should probably stay away awhile."

As they returned to their car I remembered the dagger under Gene's pillow. Not that it would make a difference, I thought, but together with the grave it would cast a more sinister light on Gene, warn of possible greater danger. A case for informing could definitely be made, but something held me back. The squatter would eventually be punished for assaulting the B&B guest, that was his due, but should I sit in judgment and sully him further? He was part of the tower's history, perhaps my father's as well, by way of Tilda which would make Gene my half-brother. Jerry's, too. This was assuming a lot, I knew, but such a thought had been nagging at me since I viewed Tilda's painting in the tower living room. The veil of secrecy around my inheritance had been in place for decades. There was no telling now what had gone on behind it.

<hr />

I followed the sheriff's advice and departed the tower, my plan to stay the night scuttled. As I sat in a restaurant having dinner, however, I became increasingly bothered by this turn in my situation. Why, I wondered, should I have my time up here disrupted by an oaf with a tree limb? I understood the sheriff's reasoning, but to cut myself off from the tower was to extend the damage already done by Gene. I felt an impulse to drive back out and decided to indulge it.

Darkness had fallen and the lesser roads near the end of my drive were completely unlit. I'd likely have given up or gotten lost if this were my first time out. As it was, I had to proceed slowly to see the turns and avoid various forest animals. My access road at the end was especially hard to see, so I was almost at the tower before I noticed something that caused me to cut the headlights and edge forward stealthily.

There was light emanating from the non-boarded lower windows.

I pulled my car into deep shadows beside the primitive road, exited without a door slam, carefully approached the tower. I avoided the front and side of the building, moved to the rear where lookout was less likely. There were sounds: night insects, clatter from the generator, scratchy country music from a broken window behind thorny rose tangle. A shadow moved inside. I backed away, watching first the broken window and then the door in front, where the new lock could be disengaged from within. Back near my car, I fished out the sheriff's card I'd been given. I hesitated to call the number on it, pondering again Gene's connection to our family, but then I recalled the broken window, the dagger under the pillow up the stairs. I pressed the buttons on my phone.

"A man wanted for assault has broken into my home," I told the night officer. "He's in there now. The sheriff was here looking for him today."

I gave him some details and my location.

"We'll be out there ASAP, sir. Stay away from the suspect. The town police might be there ahead of us."

"He might be armed, at least with a dagger."

"We'll take care of it, sir."

I got into my car and waited. The sound of insects predominated here, varied occasionally by a flutter of wings or rustle in the bushes. My feelings toward Gene hardened into irritation, resentment, almost hatred for his disruption of my trip here, my peaceful exploration of my inheritance. But there was also the inevitable guilt for having such feelings. This had been Gene's home, after all, he and Tilda making their lives here with my father's approval, his apparent participation at times. But as a legacy he'd intended the tower for me. That was clear. His obligations toward Gene were to end with his death.

In my rearview mirror I saw the lights of multiple vehicles moving in the maze of roadways. They reached the point where I'd pulled off to the side. An officer in the lead car spoke to me through our windows.

"Are you all right?" she asked when I'd identified myself.

"Yes. He hasn't seen me."

"Just stay here. We'll get back to you."

They advanced to the end of the access road, two cars and a van. The occupants got out and briefly conferred, then two officers headed toward the rear of the building with guns drawn. Three others approached the front while one remained with the vehicles. A period of quiet ensued, no burst of activity, culminating in the return of two of the officers with a handcuffed man between them. He was led to the rear of the van and placed inside with a vigorous slamming of the doors. He still hadn't seen me, but I'd observed he was somewhat short, underweight, with features looking older than I'd expected. The face was familiar, though, and shockingly so, for it was my father's face. Neither I nor Jerry showed such a close resemblance.

—————

"Are you calling from the tower, Brian?"

"No, I'm back at the motel. The police have the tower taped off."

"The police? Why's that?"

"It's a crime scene, Jerry. They need to search for evidence. In case there's more than they have already."

"I don't understand."

I related the events of the previous day, my earlier discovery of the grave, the sheriff's account of the assault, the apparent reason for it. Jerry listened without interrupting.

"They found drugs and pornography in Gene's possession when they arrested him. He has a record of other offenses."

I waited a moment for my brother to respond.

"Do you think Dad--" he began. "Well, the grave and all, do you think he had anything to do with wrongdoing there?"

"Other than just knowing the people, supporting their life there, no. Of course, there's his leading that secret life unbeknown to us or Mom."

"Especially Mom."

"Yeah, of course."

"So, what do you think you'll do with all this, Brian? The property, this character Gene?"

I hadn't yet told him of the man's startling resemblance to our father. Gene's apparent relation to us was only a vague possibility to

Jerry at this point. I saw no reason to saddle him now with another shock, likely one with unwelcome consequences.

"I'm inclined to put the place up for sale," I said. "It's not realistic to try fixing it up. It's not worth the time and expense. And I wouldn't want to live around here, even come here for a getaway. I'd like to put the whole thing behind me, squatters included."

"Seems the wind sort of went out of your sails."

"Yes. Gaining awareness can do that."

———※———

The tower and surrounding land was listed for sale by a real estate broker in the town where I stayed. Shortly thereafter, however, a fire broke out and entirely destroyed the tower's interior. The realty listing was revised to be primarily for the land, though a unique stone artifact was mentioned. The only offer subsequently received was from the neighboring B&B: one hundred dollars and closing costs. They thought the artifact might draw attention to their place and the outhouse would be handy for nature-loving guests.

I instructed the broker to accept the offer.

A SUPERIOR MAID

As a financial analyst who was respected in his community, Arnold was attentive to detail, be it with investments or his own relationships. He made a point of reaching the office at five after nine, demonstrating both dependability and license to be late. His phone calls opened with a joke or two, but after that he wanted straight, hard facts. Zero tolerance for the old horse manure, and he never dealt with public relations people.

At home, he forgot all about it. He did none of the work, inside or out, on his and Ashley's sixteen rooms. Minority lawn men roamed the grounds in summer, returning to seal the driveway in autumn, plow snow in winter, and paint the trim in springtime. A local matron handled the supper, while nymphs from an agency did the Saturday cleaning. Arnold and Ashley were free to lounge and sip, page through magazines or watch a video, anything that absorbed their mental processes. They could then go to bed conscious only of each other.

Weekends were different. Since Sunday belonged to society--church, relatives, and such--Arnold claimed Saturday as his own. He'd get up an hour later, have a workout and light breakfast, then retreat to the library. He'd stay there till evening, only coming down for a salad and muffin at midday. Ashley had learned, with effort, that Saturday was sacred to Arnold, so she never disturbed him. Arnold was left to his private work, which everyone assumed was of great importance. Actually, he was simply reviewing his personal finances or trying his hand at poetry, which he knew was futile. But it didn't matter what he did here. The point was to keep people from taking this day from him.

While Ashley accepted Arnold's strangeness, Saturday was an odd piece in the puzzle. The day-long absence, or silent presence, drained her patience. She needed an escape. So with a friend of hers, a woman in community affairs, she enrolled in an extension course. A good move, she thought, because it took her away from Arnold and the big, quiet house. Knowing his need for details, though, she felt she should explain herself.

"It's only for the fall," she said. "Late September through early December."

"What's it called?"

"'Understanding Minority Cultures.'"

"Racial and such?"

"Well, yes. Those and others. They're a big part of society now. We need to understand them better."

"Glenbowe is white, 99% anyway. There's the minister's boat kids, but that's about it."

"Well, there's a world beyond Glenbowe. You go to work in it every day. And *it* comes *here* to work."

"All for you, all for you."

"Arnold, there's bigger things involved. It'd help to know these people when you run for office. The districts are mapped--"

"When? Did you say when? Not *if* I go into politics?"

"Well, we should be prepared--when, if, whatever."

"We were talking hypothetically. Whimsically."

"You never do that. And this is only a course, Arnold. It would widen our options for the future and--well, it's something I want to do."

"Did I say you couldn't?"

"No. But we've always been together on weekends. Near each other, I mean. So I care what you think about it."

"Well, as you say, it's only one course."

She waited for him to say, "and I want you to be happy," but he didn't say it. She didn't know that a part of him was glad--a part of him that felt twinges of guilt when he avoided her on Saturdays. Of course, he'd have to watch the help somehow, keep them from stealing. But he'd never had much trouble controlling people.

The lawn men should stay outside, so Arnold decided to lock the doors and forget about them. The cook arrived at four, near the end of library time, and was chained to the kitchen by her duties. This left the maid from the agency, fluttering about the house from ten to three. Arnold phoned the agency and insisted they send the same maid for a twelve-week period, and only one of their best. Later, the agency called and said they'd found someone.

Her name, it turned out, was Una. She was tall and blond with a European accent. Arnold assumed she'd been imported as an *au pair*. She probably had Saturdays off from some CEO's estate. What better way to spend it than by cleaning a few more toilets? As he showed her around, though, he was impressed by her professionalism. She asked about every room's needs, eager to please though this was only weekly for her.

"Yes, sir," she said. "I will keep doors locked. I know must be careful of strange helpers."

"Well, it's mostly so I'm not disturbed. I have very important work to do in the library."

"What is your lunch, sir? I will bring to you?"

"I've been coming down for that."

"I can bring to you, sir. The work is so important, your time must not waste."

He felt confident of Una, satisfied with his analysis and action on the new situation. He went through the library routine in peace, and with the added anticipation of room service. She was on time to the minute, bearing the salad and muffin on an expensive tray that had hung on the wall. The vegetables were finely cut and arranged in a pattern, making them more appetizing. The butter for the muffin was formed into flowers, and Una had added jelly jars from a forgotten Christmas box.

"This is very nice," Arnold said.

"You like more, sir?"

"No, this is fine. But Una, if you remember, can you note the time the lawn men finish? I want to verify the statement they leave."

"I will write down. I know must be careful, sir."

He was undisturbed through the afternoon. Una left promptly at three o'clock, before Ashley returned. The extension course had extended through the day. When Una left, Arnold decided to inspect her work, get immediate feedback on his plan. As he went through the house, he found it cleaner than he'd ever seen it. Leaning into the four toilet bowls, he noted that even the slight rust marks had been removed.

Ashley came home after the cook arrived. He was peeved with Ashley for staying out so long, but the day had gone well after all. And even if she pulled this every week, where was the harm? He decided to gently chide her and let it go at that.

"Well," Ashley replied, "I really couldn't help it, Arnold. We had to get our books and there was library work. Later on, there'll be study groups. Then too, I don't see Monica that often so we dropped into Orly's."

"That's all right," he said. "I was only kidding."

"You were? That isn't like you."

"Well, no harm done. Anyway, it's good for you to get out once in a while--with someone else, I mean--whatever crazy stuff you're studying."

"Now, Arnold--"

"Just kidding, just kidding."

She was puzzled by his mood, but this quickly passed as she noticed the day's cleaning job. Arnold felt smug as she passed through the rooms. She had never before seen the house so perfect. She overlooked the toilet bowls, but Arnold pointed them out to her. Pristine, they agreed.

"I have to hand it to you," she said. "You always come out ahead on things."

His mood carried into the work week. He still arrived at five after nine, but he remembered Una in working with the firms. Had they checked their equipment for rust stains, he asked, or other impurities? If their product was food, was it precisely cut with extra touches for attractiveness? They might be amused by this, but it made them take the rest more seriously. His analysis knew no bounds, they'd think. He might even come nosing into toilet bowls.

The second Saturday started like the first, Ashley departing with her friend and Una arriving at ten, precisely. Arnold faded to the library, confident of the maid's efficiency. Lunch arrived to the minute again, festooned with nuts and dried fruit--treasures forgotten on a pantry shelf. He imagined he tasted Una's fingers on it, then her lips, her tongue. He chuckled as he thought of telling her this, knowing he would not.

"Lunch was delicious," he said. "I want to give you something for the extra service."

"Tip, sir? No, not good. There is agency rule."

"They'll never know."

She took the cash reluctantly. He watched as she walked to the bus stop, noting the strong motion of her hips. She was ready for anything, he thought, fresh as ever after five hours of work. And appealing, sexual--like an engine of youth renewed by action. The harder she worked, the more she was energized.

Ashley was pleased with the cleaning again, and Arnold returned to work with new inspiration. He timed his arrival to the second, bursting in with a smile at 9:05:00. He asked executives if they could taste their secretaries on their coffee cups. This unnerved them more than usual, better setting up his incisive questions. Had they thought, he asked, of simply driving their people harder? Letting their generators charge them with working power? When they mentioned unions or morale, Arnold just scoffed.

"You know," Ashley said to him, "you seem a lot bouncier this last couple of weeks. You're more fun to be with. You're building to something, I think, something bigger and better."

"Local politics? Capture the hearts of Glenbowe and vicinity?"

"For a start. We'd be great at it, Arnold. We have everything going for us."

"We're even understanding minorities."

"It won't hurt. And you'd be surprised what there is to know--how much you can use. Come on, let's invite the committeeman to dinner!"

"Could be you're right. It would be work--hard work--but it would generate power."

Ashley felt rising elation.

"You're serious?" she asked.

"I'll think about it."

When Una arrived for the third Saturday, she carried a small parcel. It was tea and a nut cake, she explained, bought with Arnold's tip. She wanted him to enjoy them while she cleaned.

"You were supposed to spend it on yourself," he said.

"Is impossible, sir. You already generous pay."

"Well, perhaps you can join me then. I never eat between meals, but come after lunch and we'll enjoy it together."

"But sir, the work. I must do cleaning."

"Just leave a window or two."

She went about her duties. Arnold spent the morning envisioning her--the powerful, churning legs, the flat fatless belly, and the fine breasts. He'd like to see her nude, he thought--do a thorough analysis of her. He started to lose patience waiting for lunch. For lunch to be over, really, so he could talk with her.

"Do you think you could call me Arnold instead of sir? I get that enough at the office."

"But I--with employer, I never do before."

"I'm different from your other employer. When you come here, you get a break from some things."

"Yes, Arnold. Is very *nice* break."

Her using his name distracted him a moment. It was perfect. He'd requested she call him Arnold and she'd done it, unabashed.

"The fact is, Una, it's a break for me, too. I admire your efficiency, consideration. I like you."

"I want you happy is all, Arnold."

"Your husband or boyfriend is very lucky, I think."

"I have none, Arnold. Am only working girl."

"But an excellent one. A special one. Why don't you leave the rest of the cleaning and stay with me till three?"

"Wife will notice, I think."

"Yes. Well, stay an hour at least. Your being here means a lot to me. I can cover for you with the wife."

She stayed until the tea was cold, smiling under Arnold's gaze. It was almost like she'd undress, Arnold thought, at his request. She hesitated on leaving, as if wanting to kiss. He knew then he must act. Next week, he thought, after meaningless days without her.

She arrived the next week with cake and tea again, Arnold wanting to reimburse her. Una would have nothing to do with it.

"Is from me to you," she said. "No price on that."

"We'll have it now, then."

"What of your work? And not eat between meals?"

"A change of priorities. Why do in three hours what's better done now?"

She went to make the tea. They stayed in a parlor this time, blinds drawn against the lawn men raking leaves. They eyed each other through hibiscus steam, ignoring a saucer of nut cake. It was clear, Arnold thought, that this was the time. He set down his cup and moved around the table, settling on the couch next to Una. She sipped her tea, faintly smiling. Heavier than Ashley, Arnold thought, but also taller. Her body heat invited his touch.

"Mind if I kiss you?" he asked.

She set down her cup, then eased back in the cushions.

"Yes, kiss," she said.

He moved in swiftly and they made love. He stayed on her when it ended, a financial expert blanket for the maid on duty. When he finally rolled off, she quickly sat up, energized again by her efforts.

"There is the cleaning," she said.

"Are you serious?"

"Wife will notice."

"Forget it. I'll help you with it later."

"You have your work, very much important."

"It's nothing, just a way to kill time."

"Oh?"

He got up and sat with her on the couch. It was different now with the passion spent, something like being with Ashley. His gaze and his thoughts became clinical, appraising. A good specimen, he thought, one he'd want again. And again and again.

"Seems she was off today," Ashley said later. "I saw a ring in the second-floor toilet."

"I'll talk to her about it," said Arnold.

"No, don't bother. Everyone has bad days. Might be family problems, for all we know. Or a *boyfriend.*"

"Yes, that might have been it. She seemed a little depressed."

"Best not to get involved."

He took her again the next week, and the week after that. Between Saturdays, he thought of Una while taking Ashley. He tried to imitate the excitement, but Ashley's writhing was no match for Una's. Unsatisfied, he'd wake her in the night to try again.

"Arnold," she complained, "you're out of control!"

But then she didn't mind, even praising his vigor. At the office, he was cockier than ever. He'd be early or late as it suited him, no longer the 9:05 Old Faithful. In making calls, there was no more need to tell jokes. Instead, he'd ask the other party to tell *him* one. And if it wasn't forthcoming, he got quick revenge.

"Your receptionist sounded nice," he'd say. "Had her in the sack lately?"

He developed a snort to accompany the remarks, making it his trademark in the office. Other men laughed and it seemed he was riding a crest. Let the committeeman come, open the gates to politics and power! Ashley could handle the minorities, use her understanding on them. She'd also help with the women's vote. But wait a minute, he thought. There was a thing on that. The office secretaries were bugged by his new attitude. His snort made them nervous, his stares more so. The president was aware but hadn't yet spoken to him about it. Arnold was too good with investors. But details could get out of hand, boomerang on him. And leading them, he suddenly saw, would be Una.

That Saturday, the first in November, was drizzly and cold. It should have been cozy in the brass four-poster, but Arnold was bothered. Una was smothering him as usual, but his reaction was mechanical. Una was just a facility for him, like a urinal. He tried to act normal and helped with the cleaning, but knew he'd have to change something. When Saturday came again, he decided, he had to stop this.

"We can't do that today," he said the next week.

"Not do? What is you mean, Arnold?"

"Things have changed. We have to slow down a bit."

"You are sick?"

"No, not sick."

They were sitting in the second-floor parlor where, four weeks past, he'd first taken her. As he stared into space holding teacup on knee, Una unbuttoned her dress. She sat within reach, but he only glanced at her.

"Touch me, Arnold. I want you caress me."

He briefly stroked her leg, patting her knee as he finished. She moved in close and he could smell her. As he put down his tea, her hand advanced to him. He caught her wrist.

"No," he said, "not today."

She looked at him quizzically, then withdrew and buttoned her dress. Arnold recovered his teacup.

"You will have the lunch?" she asked.

"Yes, if you don't mind."

The tea was finished and they went their separate ways. Arnold felt awkward in the library, editing once again his pseudo-poetry. Una might be resentful, he knew, and this would be aggravated by having to scrub his toilets. He had to be careful and keep her under control. He couldn't afford any outbursts here.

"Sorry about today," he said later. "We'll talk about it next week."

She was late the next week and didn't bring goodies. Arnold didn't care; he and Ashley would be gone the next week for Thanksgiving. It would be a break in these meetings, with only two Saturdays beyond it. He'd again resist Una today, then let Thanksgiving take over.

"You want the brass bed today?" she asked.

"No, Una. Not today."

"Is a problem, Arnold?"

"Yes. Same as last week, I'm afraid. More serious even."

"What problem is it? You said we talk."

"Yes, I did."

Una sat on the edge of her chair, lips parted. She hadn't done any cleaning yet.

"You know I'm married," Arnold said. "Ashley will be staying home in a few weeks so, obviously, we can't go on."

"Just meet another place, Arnold."

"Another place?"

He thought about it, was tempted, found it too complicated.

"No, I can't do that."

"Why no?"

"Una, look. It's been fun with you, a nice experience. But we have to call it quits now. I have no other way. What I'd like to do is give you a gift, something to sort of--"

"I am just *whore* to you, Arnold?"

"I didn't mean it that way," he said. "I just wanted to end things in a way--"

"End things? Why we must end things? You don't like good sex? What you will do now--go back with the poetry? Sit and kill the time? Is that what you want until time to die?"

Her assertiveness gave her added beauty. He didn't have an answer, yet he had to say something.

"It's not that I don't want you. It's just that--well, I can't have you. My life is set up, see--"

With a controlled, graceful rush, she was on him. She covered him with kisses as he slumped in the couch. Hugging her, meaning to control her, he found he couldn't. He clung to her as he'd clung to the past, for comfort against all that threatened him.

"We go the brass bed now?"

"Yes, we go."

Thanksgiving was no relief. Two hundred miles from home, awash in rustic fun, his view of her never faded. Three times one night, then four the next, he tried to erase her with Ashley. Tried to reinstate the old world order. Ashley wasn't enough, though, and even started to resent him.

"You're getting sadistic," she said. "It was nice at first but you're making it nasty, hurting me. I need to sleep, Arnold."

He thought of his gun in the game room closet. He thought how he could cover the taste of poison with almond flavored tea. He saw himself choking Una, but then her throwing him off with her servant strength. He saw them both in the woods, a bridge over the river. A quick, smooth heave and she was in the water, through the ice and ready to be frozen in, covered by snowfall.

No, he thought, it wasn't worth it. Besides the enormous risks, there must surely be a simple solution.

Then one hit him: a lockout. He was Una's employer, the lord of the premises. If he chose to not admit her, to suspend her employment, she'd have no chance to further complicate his life. When the agency complained, he'd pay their bill and tell them to quit sending her. What could she say to anyone? It had to be the answer.

He watched her coming up the walk at ten the next Saturday. She was eager and had the goodies again. What she met at the door was a blank face, centered in a foot-square window. A Christmas wreath surrounded window and face, making Una smile. She gestured for Arnold to open the door, doing a mock shiver to emphasize the weather. The face before her rotated from side to side. She repeated her pantomime; Arnold repeated his turndown. He paid no attention as she started speaking, then shouting. He let her stamp about, then went to another room, waiting. The doorbell rang a few times, then stopped. When he checked back at the door, he saw she'd left.

As he was finishing lunch he heard the doorbell again. He automatically ignored it. But when he checked a short time later, he noticed an envelope below the mail slot. Knowing it was from Una, he opened it and read:

Dear Jerk,
You think you dump me but not so easy. I told you not whore but you pay now. Pay for crime. I can tell wife, tell business, tell everybody. At 10 a.m. next Saturday I coming. We talk then how you will pay. Lock the door and you are ruined. By the way I have video of us. My compact was a mini-cam by big brass bed.

The note was typed and unsigned, useless should he call the police. But that, he knew, was hardly an option for him. He'd only ruin himself instead of having her do it.

During the intervening week he cleaned his gun. Too late now for the other methods, he thought. Even this one was risky with that video floating around. But he was a master of detail and she was an immigrant servant. With proper disposal of the body, no one would be suspicious. They'd think she was running out on her work contract, returning to the old country maybe. If the video turned up, no one would care who the naked man was. One of her own type, they'd think--a blue-collar boy with a taste for the kinky.

"Where shall we talk?" he asked that Saturday.

"Is good enough by door here."

"Don't you want to sit down at least, take off your coat?"

"Time is gone for take off clothes."

"All right."

He watched her standing in the foyer, awaited her demands with his customary blank face. This would be a great place to drop her, he thought, her blood on the tiles an easy wipe-up. As he stared at her, Una's eyes tightened with anger.

"One thousand by Christmas," she said. "After that we see."

"When do I get the video?"

"You not get."

"So how do I know you have one?"

"You can have the copy, but not made yet."

He showed her his office smile.

"Without the video, I pay nothing."

She frowned, glancing toward the door. Arnold figured he'd shaken her.

"I will talk," she said, "tell everyone. When they want proof I have the video."

There was no other way, Arnold thought. He was fully justified in killing her. He slid the gun out of his coat and held it on her. It felt cool in his hand, an instrument of control. Una spoke quickly.

"Rupert is out there."

"Bullcrap."

"You look out. See yourself. He to call police after ten minutes."

Arnold backed to a curtain. Peeking out, he saw a car parked on the street. Its motor was running and a man in stocking cap was watching the house. He was husky, unmoving.

"So," she said, "no bullcrap, right?"

Arnold kept the gun on her, thinking. What if he let her go? No police complaint; she had nothing to gain by it. But now there was Rupert, demands for cash, a royal pain in his life. Yet he couldn't shoot her now; he'd never get away with it. He lowered the gun and replaced it in his coat.

"I have the small paper for you," she said, "box number address. Put just cash, Arnold, and please not show through envelope."

He took it from her. He knew his face showed contempt, but he couldn't control it.

"You're a whore," he told her.

Una just laughed.

"And what you are, Arnold? Customer of the whore? So now you pay, right? Nothing is free!"

She laughed again as she opened the door. Arnold drew the gun as she walked from the house. He could take them *both* out, he thought, say they tried to rob him. But no, said a voice deeper in, that isn't a right analysis. The game is over and you need to walk away. You've lost almost all, but you still have your freedom. With time, you'll find a way to beat them. You're the master of details, after all. Those people are no match for you.

The car pulled away and was gone down the street.

PROPERTY LINES

Even before his leopard-skin loincloth was delivered, Arthur was making his midnight rounds. He'd walk along the boundaries of the properties, meeting only the occasional cat, as he studied the backyards and windows of his bourgeois neighbors. He could range for blocks since he was sly crossing streets. And that was where the appeal lay, after all: being unseen while yet he was seeing. It gave him a sense of power to balance his usual vulnerability, the scrutiny he received at the office, on the train, and in his home. He was master of the night during this pre-sleep interlude.

It had begun as a simple stroll when Kris would go to bed early. She'd been put on full-time at the arboretum, working in the herbarium, and she took her work very seriously. The arbitrary bedtime with Arthur had to be sacrificed. He remained in his old late-night pattern, not wishing to change, and filled the void of her absence with mundane activities. Hence arose his walk to take the night air, first up and down the street but soon shifting to less conventional, aberrant routes.

It occurred to him early on, when he left the street to walk the rear boundaries of yards, that he needn't take care in dressing as he usually did. Indeed, it might be better if he weren't recognizable. Not that he was likely to be seen. He could probably wear anything without encountering problems, even go nude. He wouldn't go *that* far, of course. But it would add to the thrill, the sense of control, if his garb were something unusual, daring, an implied challenge to the normal world. Thus came to mind the loincloth. He shopped for it online, chose leopard over zebra pattern, had it shipped to his private mailbox.

With Kris off on errands one Saturday, he stood before a full-length mirror in his new garment. He liked what he saw. Though he didn't work out much, he had a naturally strong-looking build. The effect was diminished by his high brow and glasses, but overall he presented a good closet Tarzan. He couldn't resist striking a few poses.

The first night he wore it he did not venture far. His neighbors to either side were of little interest, so he softly strode to the distant rear boundary of his lot, stood among trees and bushes facing the property behind. Across their backyard, in a lighted upstairs window, a high school girl was wont to change her clothes and do exercises in a topless state. He watched now as she prepared for bed, exercise apparently over. He reflected on a discovery he'd made long before: many young women off the ground floor will not bother to cover their windows when they undress. As if no one might be looking up from a distance, or peering at them through binoculars from across the yards. Which Arthur did, of course.

The girl's light went out and he ducked into the foliage. He considered which direction to take along the property lines. To the north he'd come to an eyesore of a house with a worse eyesore of a garage, an embarrassment to the neighborhood. An old man lived there, often doing something with power tools in the garage. Arthur had never spoken with him but enjoyed snooping there, seeing what the old man was up to, whether he was sober or drunk, alive or dead. But then there were the feral cats who lived in a refuse pile there, a legacy of the man's late wife. They might not react calmly to the leopard skin, sometimes were nasty, did things as a pack. Arthur decided he'd prowl to the south instead.

He passed along the quiet yards, occasionally disturbing small animals, hearing the song of insects, night birds, frogs of some sort. At the end of his block was a rustic-looking house with wagon wheels and such decorating the yard. Arthur had noticed numerous men, restless and confused in appearance, living here for brief periods. They would often be seated at a picnic table beneath a huge oak tree, having animated discussions. It was apparently a "halfway house" of some sort. No one was out just now, though, so Arthur could trot across the adjacent road with easy secrecy. Anyone spotting him from afar would assume he was one of the drifters.

He crossed diagonally across an expansive church property. Across the lawns and parking lots he saw a light burning in the 24-hour chapel, which was a wing of the main church. There would be one or two worshipers in it, since it was always supposed to be manned, but he'd like to enter it some night. He envisioned himself on the cross, hanging there in his loincloth, caressed by the gentle holy lights. Perhaps a time when no one showed up, with a mask of some sort just in case. To be seen but not identified would be okay. It might even enhance his enjoyment, his sense of power without accountability. But this was just his first night in the loincloth. He mustn't go too far.

He passed from the church property onto the grounds of a religious high school. He wouldn't visit the school itself, which was likely full of security devices, but instead approached the "brothers' residence," where several religious faculty members lived. It was a simple one-story structure, and he saw that two of the four men were still up. One was the principal, whom Arthur had spotted in a local casino and dubbed Brother Ace. The other was an aloof, studious man he thought of as Brother Hubert. Having retired for the night, apparently, were Brother Tuck, a heavy eater, and Brother Ichabod, who seemed the oldest but dragged himself through long distance runs in all weather. Arthur decided to avoid Brother Ace but spy a bit on Brother Hubert, who was several rooms away.

He crouched on the ground facing Hubert's window, which was on the corner of the building nearest the school. Through partially closed blinds flashed multicolored light from a television screen. Arthur discerned a profile of the brother's face, rapt in the illumination. Perhaps he was watching porn, Arthur considered. He found a small stone in the grass and sent it in a high, soft arc toward Hubert's window. It glanced off with a nice click, anomalous in the quiet suburban night. The brother reacted quickly, coming to the window and peeking through the blinds, then raising them for a panoramic view. But Arthur was lying face-down, invisible in the darkness. As Hubert turned away to extinguish his light, the man in the loincloth slipped away, leaving only pure darkness for the view from the window.

He felt quite a lift at work the next day. Not only was life balanced by his nightly excursions, but he'd actually gained an edge on those scrutinizers who tormented him. The leopard-skin loincloth gave him an identity–additional to the activity–that his adversaries knew nothing about. What they scrutinized was meaningless now since his real life, his real self, lay in the night. They noticed his new lightness of manner, adding notes of collegiality to the respect owed his knowledge of finance. Even on the commuter train, where he'd ridden as an anonymous stiff, he now felt on a par with the men who exuded prosperity. He could match their ease of manner and relate with them. He even decided to pick up a roll of quarters so he could flip them to the panhandlers.

In the ensuing nights he steadily expanded his roaming range. He crossed streets at the dark spots, where lighting was weakest, and kept as much as possible to the rear property lines. He'd always carried treats for any dogs left out at night, but to these he now added pepper spray. The loincloth required more insurance against discovery. At some point, of course, he might *want* to be seen, to exhibit his persona, but it had to be planned and yield no clue to his daylight identity. Friday and Saturday nights he stayed home, Kris staying up later since she wasn't rising early for work. Arthur didn't mind since it made his rounds all the sweeter when he resumed them.

"You've been rather chipper lately," she said.

"Have I?"

"Yes. Good news at the firm?"

"Nothing that matters financially. Minor staff changes. More tolerable group now."

They were having tuna casserole, his favorite among Kris's entrees.

"You know, Arthur, I appreciate your adjustment. And I'm impressed by it."

"The night schedule, you mean?"

"Yes. You don't get too bored, do you? Or lonely? You find enough to do?"

He shrugged.

"Always something doing on the Internet."

"Like what, for instance?"

She always had to complicate things, he thought, couldn't leave well enough alone.

"Oh," he replied, "the *Journal*, online edition."

"But don't you read it on the train?"

"Well, I've been talking more with my fellow passengers. Getting sociable. Part of feeling chipper, I guess."

"Oh, that's nice. That's *great*, Arthur!"

Actually, he'd been catching up on his sleep when he commuted. While he was disciplined in his forays, they often took him past a normal bedtime. Kris, a deep sleeper, was none the wiser, but a second life simply had to impact his first one. Rather than having oodles of time to read business news, he now had none. But he need not read the *Journal* to do his work, he thought, for he relied mostly on instinct now, anyway. This was consistent with his life and attitude in the leopard-skin loincloth.

One night he ventured beyond the brothers' residence and their academy to the spacious grounds of the local public high school. The large building on the far end had security lighting, but the long stretch of athletic fields did not. Arthur could walk freely in the open, inhale the night's fragrance, listen to night sounds near and far. He tested a rubberized running track, stood atop a pitcher's mound with arms akimbo. King of the hill, he reflected. As he was moving on, however, toward the enclosed football field with its bleachers, he thought he heard a voice or two in the distance, and a giggle. Had he been seen? He crouched low and searched the night in all directions. When again he heard a voice–a girl's–he focused on its direction and spotted an anomaly in the shadows beneath the bleachers. There were people on the ground–a couple and two or three others more distant–occupied with each other and smoking. He had not been seen. He felt relief, but resolved to be more careful in the future. To be scrutinized in this second life would defeat its essential purpose.

Kris had little awareness of his sensitivity to attention. She took their marriage for granted, as being without issues, which freed her to do as she wished. This was why Arthur had married her, to balance and assuage his life under a micromanaging mother. He'd been her firstborn, suffering her constant corrections while his younger brother went scot-free. Their folksy father could not correct the situation. But now, with Kris, Arthur had a buffer against all that. She was plain and rather bony, inclined to speak in a monotone, but he'd accepted her as the best of his possible matches in a world of unwelcome people.

There was a man on the train, Alec, who'd taken some advantage of Arthur's lighter manner. The catch-up nap was often disrupted by Alec's litany of complaints about his job, his family, and modern society. Disturbed in this way one morning, Arthur was inspired to respond frankly from his new perspective, to proselytize.

"Maybe you need another life," he said.

"Another life?"

"Yes. Something completely separate from what you've got now."

Alec gave him a puzzled look.

"You mean just take off? Ditch it all and start over?"

"No, you keep it all, or most of it. But you add something, a nice pleasant routine, probably in secret. A private second life."

The other man stared into space, considering. His stunned conventional features, Arthur thought, bespoke the ignorance of middle-class working men. They had been brainwashed by their culture.

"What *kind* of second life?" Alec asked.

"That's up to you. Could be anything, just so it's sustainable and you enjoy it."

"We're not talking mistress here, are we?" A wink. "Or is it just a secret fishing hole?"

"It *is* best to keep things simple. After all, it has to fit in with your usual life, and secretly." Arthur paused, becoming cautious. "Let me tell you about a guy I met, one who did what I'm talking about. He started with just a walk."

"A walk?"

"One that became very special, evolved."

He related his own history of late-night perambulation, converting to third person and omitting identifying details. He tried to affect a monotone, not show how much he relished some parts, hoping his eyes or body language didn't betray him. But he soon saw that he needn't be concerned. Alec tended to look away as if trying to picture things, smiling in the comfort of vicarious enjoyment.

"That's some yarn," he commented. "You believe the guy?"

Arthur shrugged.

"He seemed candid enough. Of course, I don't know him well."

Alec looked away again.

"I don't know. All that seems sort of–well, extreme. I mean, I can see what you're talking about, the carving out personal space and all. But I don't want to get branded a nut. Secrets get found out, after all. Then what do you do?"

Arthur didn't hazard an answer. For himself, the risk was part of the thrill, and he was confident he could keep it all secret. But his seatmate wasn't cut from the same cloth as he, could never be as daring or resourceful. And neither could the other men on this train. This reinforced for Arthur the specialness, the exclusivity, of the persona he had created for himself. He was one of a kind.

Most people, he saw, could not even appreciate what he'd accomplished. They'd consider him a "nut," as Alec had implied. Nonetheless, Arthur felt an urge to display his second self, to have its existence affirmed by being witnessed. He'd abandoned one such plan, the hanging on the cross in the 24-hour chapel. The indoor exposure was too risky; the lighting and hindered escape would endanger his first identity. What he desired was a sort of flash appearance, like the split-second scenes in a movie or TV preview. He'd expanded his roaming to several blocks in each direction, so he would choose the best spot within that radius.

To the west of the high schools and somewhat north, beyond another zone of housing, lay a large public park. It was bounded on two sides by major streets. Arthur approached along rear property lines, as usual, but also felt safe on the narrow, shaded side streets. The park itself was a sudden change. Unlike the high school grounds, there were lights on tall poles over the whole space. Arthur hesitated on the fringe, still among bushes, and surveyed the scene. Traffic was light at this hour on the intersecting streets, but there were cars in the parking lot. He saw two people on the grass in the center of the park, another couple to the north, someone walking a dog along the street to the west, and a man drinking behind the park building. Arthur snapped clip-on sunglasses over his horn-rims, took a breath, and trotted lightly into the open parkland.

Keeping to the east side of the park, he passed the young man and woman in its center. She seemed to not notice him while her boyfriend stared blankly. Arthur passed in and out of the high lighting, trying to sustain his faun-like trot, avoid a sprint or desultory jog. As he approached the north end of the park, he could see he'd been noticed there by the second couple. They'd looked up from their tete-a-tete and the man was grinning in amusement. Arthur turned toward the west before he reached them.

"Aw, c'mon," he heard the man say.

Arthur concentrated on his pace, on his feet in the grass.

"Hey, fairy!" the man shouted behind him.

Arthur inwardly flinched.

"Fairy!" came the voice once more.

The western side of the park was near, the dog-walker discreetly glancing over, his dog disinterested. Arthur made the turn to trot south, scanning the car traffic for reactions. There were none. He was a lone, graceful runner, his second self asserting its viability. He clung to his pride in this, telling himself that the shouter had just been an idiot. The flicker of irritation would soon pass. Yet he wasn't quite focused as he approached the southern park area, the building and the parking lot beyond. The drinking man had been sitting but was now standing, staring fixedly at this man in leopard-skin and sunglasses. Arthur made his turn to the east and heard some bitter grumbling, fortunately unintelligible. The sentiment was clear, however, piercing the night like a growl from a lower animal. He should dismiss it as such, Arthur knew, but it served to reinforce the pejorative from before, with the evident consensus on him one of disgust.

He entered some bushes on the eastern fringe of the park, feeling relief above all else.

He tried to smile on the dark trek home, take pride in his venture, but his thoughts became confused. Had there been signs from others despite his secrecy? Alec on the train had not been seeking him out lately, ever since Arthur's story of "a guy's" second life. The other regulars in the car had also become distant toward him. People at the office had seemed friendly enough, but were they patronizing him? Even Kris he couldn't be sure of. *Especially* Kris, who had the most opportunity to scrutinize him. But he mustn't get carried away, Arthur knew. A gate had been opened to self-doubt, but it needn't become a floodgate. He had to stay in control.

The next day he was cautious toward people, cool in manner, no longer interested in their fellowship or acceptance. With Kris he tried to relax, appear normal, but he was still wary. Her early-to-bed routine was especially welcome. Left on his own, Arthur had a mental picture of his leopard-skin loincloth, folded into its hiding place among the heating and cooling ducts in the utility room. It would have to remain there this night, no matter his frustration. Risk management required a night of abstention.

Needing an alternate diversion, Arthur dismissed the television as too passive. Likewise reading the *Journal*, though he'd anyhow stopped relying on it. He sat at the computer and logged on to the Internet, where something was always doing as he had assured Kris. But he found that shocks and celebrities, and what passed for interaction, were woefully inferior to his physical transport through the night. Virtual reality lacked virtue. Restless, he surfed without purpose until he recalled the high school girl in the house to the rear. He logged off.

Bathroom door locked, lights off, Arthur stepped into the dry bathtub and cranked open the small vent window. He raised his powerful binoculars and adjusted the focus. There she was. A slow smile crossed his face as he viewed her crossings of the room, her holding up garments against her body as she posed before a mirror. The only garment she actually wore was a pair of black panties. *Shiny* black, Arthur observed, with a lacy frill of some sort. He hadn't seen those before. The girl also posed without holding the garments, viewing her trim young body in profile. And she did exercises. Arthur's favorite was when she faced the window and swung a pair of steel clubs at her sides, raising knees high as she marched in place. He felt intimate with her then, her magnified image directly facing him, both she and he smiling joyfully.

After a time the girl slipped downward, out of Arthur's sight, for some activity on the floor. He'd sometimes watch until she went to bed, but these drop-downs could last a long time so he often quit on them. This would be one of those nights, he decided. He cranked shut the vent window and retreated from the bathtub. He felt a residual pleasure, though not of course the catharsis of his prowls.

The following day was a Thursday. Arthur passed the workday feeling hollow, missing the rejuvenation he'd come to expect for his days at the office. The coming night would be his last chance that week to experience his second life. He had to make it count. It suddenly occurred to him, on this score, that he might be developing a dependency. The walks as they progressed had seemed a wonderful addition to his existence, another dimension. But he wondered whether, rather than being a pure supplement, his loincloth life was filling a void, some deficiency in his character or personality. He might have been aware of it at some level, felt a need. His secret life would not then be an enhancement, but a cover for a defect. And yet, from the beginning, he'd felt drawn to it instinctively. Whatever self-knowledge existed in some remote portion of his brain, whatever level of dependency there was, he had to trust in his instinct. It wasn't perfect but it had served pretty well and was his surest guide for now. The long run could be faced later.

That night, Arthur's resolve was firm as he donned the loincloth in his downstairs utility room. He felt strong as he ascended the dark stairwell outside. As he crossed the backyard, however, the late-hour air was somehow less familiar to him. It seemed his absence of the night before had loosened his control of the night, opened it to new possibilities. He stood at the property line with less than his usual confidence. He'd compromise this night, he thought. He'd modify his prowl to observe the closer limits of before. Perhaps another visit to the brothers, a check on Brother Hubert with his porn shows. But no, that wouldn't be enough. Too tame and repetitious. Now, Brother Ace would be a different story. Poring over his racing forms for the next day, maybe on the phone with Vegas or his bookie, or absorbed in an online poker game. But how would Ace react if he saw Arthur peeking in? Not with Brother Hubert's gentility. There was money at stake, after all, and he might well have a gun.

Arthur decided to take the opposite direction, visit the hovel of the old man with its colony of feral cats. As he passed between the yards he felt curiously out of place, familiar with all he saw and yet foreign to it, until he questioned his own feelings, their relevance and even their reality. Had the value of his secret life depended upon illusion? He steadied himself, concentrating on the grass beneath his feet, which grew sparse at the edge of the old man's yard. Ahead was the shadowy refuse heap, two or three pairs of eyes glowing from it. Arthur slowed and stopped. There was movement toward the rear of the heap and he sensed four of them now, perhaps five. He felt that he'd come, unexpectedly but not tragically, to a fateful moment, a time of decision. Yet he was still unthinking, still trusting to instinct. He removed the small carry-pouch from his waist, gripped the top edge of his loincloth, and lowered it past his knees. He stepped out of it. He held the garment tentatively a moment, then flung it in a soft arc onto the refuse heap. The front cat flinched but none immediately moved. Arthur was gone before they could feel threatened.

He returned to the house with more than his usual stealth. A tinge of embarrassment struck as he crossed his backyard to the dark stairwell. It was clearly over, he realized. After dressing he made himself a drink and sat in the large den next to the utility room. Since the house was a split-level, the sleeping Kris lay one and a half stories up. Arthur felt an urge to join her, to put this night–all these nights–behind him. But he had to hold off, he knew, and be there at the expected time. There must be nothing unusual to arouse attention. One thing could lead to another until it all came out. He must be guided now by his intellect.

The weekend came as a welcome respite, rather than the interruption it had lately been. He was solicitous toward Kris, complimenting her mushroom souffle and sitting without complaint through a corny movie she selected. On Sunday she brought him to the herbarium and he easily feigned interest. There was a trendy restaurant in the arboretum proper, its windows overlooking the lagoon and surrounding plant collection, trees filling the middle distance. They sat across from each other with the view of manicured nature beside them.

"We should do this more often," Kris said, "or things like it."

"Yes," Arthur agreed, "we should."

"How did we get away from it, anyway? The little plays, the music, the drives up north. The wondrous life."

Time went by, Arthur thought, and we're not the same people. But that wouldn't do for an answer.

"There was work," he said. "Relatives. Projects at home."

But that didn't seem to do, either. She was looking out over the lagoon, her face still, thoughts perhaps drifting into useless, dangerous territory. Why should there only be the two of them? Why hadn't they tried again after their catastrophe?

"Anyway," he said, "we're here now. This beautiful setting."

"Yes," Kris answered, "here we are."

Arthur resumed his habit of picking up the *Journal* and reading it on the train. At the office he became again the bland master of finance, neither gregarious nor aloof. In the late evenings he gravitated to the home computer. He knew this was a banal response to things, at some level not respecting himself for it, but it was a safe alternative to his old reckless sallies. It was a haven, which was something his life in general now required: a rock-hard shell of protection.

He'd lived with this resolve for several days when he received a package in his office at work. It was in a postal service box and had been sent by overnight mail. The postmark was from the suburb in which he lived, but–even more oddly–the return address was his own, minus the name. Arthur examined the box and shook it but could determine nothing. At length he opened it.

The contents were cushioned and covered by tissue paper, as if they were a heartfelt gift. Spreading the tissue aside, Arthur saw his leopard-skin loincloth, neatly folded. The cats had done little or no damage. A small note, folded once, was pinned to the loincloth, the word *You* inscribed on the visible side. It was in a delicate, unfamiliar hand. Arthur unpinned the note and opened it.

Tonight, it read, *the back-yard border.* An apparent signature: *Your Performer,* followed by *P.S.—Don't throw these away.*

Within the tempest, Arthur remained calm, concentrating. His *performer,* as he'd become hers. His actions on her "smart phone," probably. His work address via the Internet, using his name from public property records. Or maybe Kris blabbed to the parents. But why did the girl say "these?" Why use that word? And no mention of money, so what did she want? Maybe there was another note–

He picked up the leopard-skin loincloth, letting the folds fall out, and with them a pair of shiny black panties with a lacy frill.

Arthur sat stunned a moment, then hastily concealed the garments.

THE LAKE ISLE

I was already 53 years of age by the time my youngest sister was born. We weren't actually blood relatives, but my widowed stepmother had remarried and borne the girl at age 44. We'd shared my father's house following his death and, until her remarriage, my stepmother had met my needs in my fated bachelorhood. It was thus rather similar to an actual mother and child relationship, despite my clear seniority. With the coming of little Magdalene, it was as if I'd gained a half-sister, or sister for short when people simplify. I'd moved to a small apartment to accommodate the husband but Laura and I remained in close contact.

Perhaps because of her mother's age at childbirth, Magdalene had delays in her development. Laura agreed with her husband, Sammy, that they should move from the old neighborhood to an area with better resources to meet their child's needs. Sammy took charge and found a promising new location. I was disappointed that it was almost 200 miles away, but Magdalene's needs took priority so I swallowed my feelings and raised no objection. It wasn't my place to do so anyway, of course, nor to suggest that Sammy would like to be rid of me. Laura made a point of assuring me that I'd always be welcome to visit them.

Then, sometime after they'd moved, she called while I was in a funk.

"We'd love to have you up here," she said. "Magdalene has been asking about you. We have the guest room all ready."

My heart accelerated at the prospect.

"You think it would be okay? With Sammy and all, I mean?"

"Of course! He misses you, too. We all do."

She was a sweet, optimistic woman, so of course I was wary of her assessment. But she'd always been an inspiration to me, I trusted her, and I greatly missed her and Magdalene. So, I agreed to go and visit come hell or high water.

———※———

I'd made a wrong turn. That was obvious now. The overarching trees, blocking the sunlight of moments before, the frequent dips and rises in the road--undulations--and its damp clay surface, the color a sickening yellow-brown--all of it warned that I was losing my way. And yet I drove on, trusting that a cross street would present itself and take me again in the direction I'd been heading. But I drove and drove and met no such street. The already struggling daylight was expiring into gloom. The forest sounds segued into a haunting timbre.

Suddenly, at the edge of the road ahead, a small sign:

Lake of Fire
2 mi.

I continued on at the same cautious speed. The road was more level now but slightly declining, the forest eventually pulling away from it to reveal the forlorn town. Most of the houses were dark, some boarded up, though I passed a nicer one with soft lighting. Further along, I sighted a little girl playing by herself outside a trailer home, then two young men inspecting a rifle on the porch of their cottage. I went through a cluster of businesses no longer in business and another stretch of mostly darkness. The town had almost slipped behind me when I came upon an oasis of normal lighting at its edge. A tall wooden sign welcomed me at the roadside:

Live Bait
All Smokes
Beer & Booze
Chocolate Soda

I pulled in and parked in front of a gas pump of 1940s vintage. It was red and had a green twin with a *No Diesel* sign hung on it. The clapboard shed beyond might once have been a family home but now showed decades of conversion to an all-services small business. Firewood, tools, barrels, crates, and assorted junk were in profusion.

A short, stocky man with white whiskers and battered hat came around a pickup truck off to the side. He was wearing oil-stained overalls and heavy work boots.

"Welcome, traveler!"

"Hi," I answered. "You're the proprietor?"

"Sure am. Mayor, too. Got all fifteen votes last time. Few abstentions of course. Some folks don't understand civic duty. Fill'er up for ye?"

"Yes, if you will. I've been driving quite a ways along your road here but seem to have lost my bearings. I was expecting to meet a crossroad going north again."

"Oh, you won't get that till you hit Dooleyville, another 25 miles or so. Road's no good in the dark, though. Pitch black, with bears and bobcats layin' at every slowdown--and there's lots of'em as maybe you noticed."

He was getting my gas. He'd had to unlock the pump, which seemed odd to me in this location. I'd have thought fifteen to twenty citizens could afford to trust each other.

"This is your only road?" I asked weakly.

"Yep."

He was watching the pump handle, not meeting my stare, apparently unaware of my nascent distress.

"So all your supplies, for all your needs, can only come in by this road? Besides it being your only way out?"

"No, not at all," he chuckled. "We have our river. Walking distance out yonder."

He gave a head jerk toward the woods.

"It's navigable?"

"Sure. Nice gentle current. Predictable."

"I don't think I crossed it on my way here."

"We're on a loop. It swings back t'other way just past town. Might be why they built it here, easy landing. Place went bust long time ago, though. Now mostly hunters and Holy Joe retreaters come through. Reminds me I gotta clean up the hostel for'em. Hunters left it in a shambles. Too bad it ain't done or you could stay in it tonight."

As he spoke he'd finished filling my tank.

"You really think I shouldn't drive on now?"

He didn't answer but looked off into the darkness. There came a distant howl, coyote or wolf. His eyes met mine again.

"Tell you what. There's this place on the river, in it really, on an island in the middle of the widening. I hold it for a lady college teacher in the city, but she won't be back till after Easter. I can let you have it for tonight, say 25 bucks, then you can drive off safe in the morning."

I thought this over, stalled a bit by asking about the teacher, how her rental situation had come about. The proprietor explained that she'd lived in the town since childhood, her mother bringing her there in a withdrawal from society, from all societies. The girl had shown great talent as an artist and musician, went off to college to study in those areas. She'd gotten caught up in the issues of the times and switched her focus to social studies. She traveled about the country and the world, immersing herself in cultures and politics as a postgraduate, but then suddenly lost interest. She took her master's degree and returned to Lake of Fire, lived with her mother in the cottage on the island. She took the teaching job when her mother died but still stayed in the cottage when classes weren't in session.

"I don't charge her for when she's gone," the proprietor added, "with the understandin' I can let it out then. 'Course I'm mighty careful who I rent to. No hunters or hippies and such. And there's an Indian girl does some light cleaning and chases the varmints away."

I found myself becoming interested. It would only be for a night and the man's travel advice was well taken. It might also enhance the story I'd be telling Laura.

"Okay," I said, "25 bucks it is."

"Fine. Just pull your car up by the pickup and get your gear. I'll walk you down to the dinghy."

As we took the well-trodden path down to the river, the proprietor explained that the teacher, when away on her job, was allowed to keep one room specially locked to protect her possessions inside. It slightly limited the rental value of the place, but he did it out of respect for her and her mother, both of whom he considered high quality people despite some aloofness.

"Much more in the mother," he was quick to add.

"Any idea what caused it?"

"She never said, I never asked. We just stuck to business."

We came to the water's edge where a small pier extended out through the cattails. An old rowboat was tied to it awaiting my boarding. The dark form of the island loomed in the distance, the shape of the cottage submerged in shadow.

"It's really a river island," said the proprietor, "but we call it our lake isle to go with the town name. 'Isle' instead of 'island' just a custom, I guess. Olden times."

I struck off through the placid water. The creak of oars and a soft rippling were the only sounds, the quiet of surrounding forest seeming to press against me. I couldn't see it in any detail, the only light being from the stars and a dim glow from distant sources. I rowed slowly in deference to my age and the usual cautions. Though I exercised daily, including use of dumbbells, the particular motions and effort of rowing were unfamiliar to my body. Hence I yielded to the reality of aging, my concessions piling up with the years.

I reached the island and beached the dinghy near a collapsed pier and two old canoes lying amidst weeds. There was a cinder path leading into the trees, pitch dark after a few steps, no signs or other guidance. I found a stout stick and waved it before me to find access and avoid obstacles. After some stumbling I came upon the cottage, larger than I'd expected and walled in by trees on all sides.

The proprietor had lent me a key and I used it to gain access. Lighting inside was weak but adequate, revealing old-fashioned furniture and frayed carpets, commonplace art prints, an outdated globe on wooden stand. In the kitchen the refrigerator was empty except for water bottles and some chocolate bars, but the cabinets held a variety of staples. There was an interesting selection of exotic teas. I selected the most substantial of the soups for my supper, along with some tasty-looking crackers.

Sitting in the living room later, sipping the brandy I'd brought, I reflected on my presence in this peaceful, time-worn setting. Many of the people I'd known well in life, souls I could picture filling seats in this room, had passed into death or hopeless oblivion. I myself was fortunate, alive and still aware, albeit in this musty isolation. There was no substitute for life. Of course, a time of reckoning would come for me also, but not just yet. Not yet. No, that was the key. The meaning of things. And to know it, to be aware, then to become indifferent. To know there was nothing you could do, so relax. Just relax. Let the memories happen, harmless and meaningless now. Just random thoughts, almost the same as dreams. Just dreams.

I awoke in the dark. What had happened? Why was the light out? I should be in one of the bedrooms upstairs, not in a chair down here. But I continued to sit there.

I awoke again. A dim light issued forth from the kitchen. Was there a shadow that had moved? I started to get up, but I'd looked away from the light and looking back did not see it. Instead there was a glow from outside as if a full moon had risen. I went to a window and peered out. My recollections returned of people I'd known, some I'd loved, their images vivid as if they were emerging from the surrounding forest. I recalled our situations and incidents, the enclosing histories of those times, stages of collapse in our culture. So much that was important, even precious, had fallen into dust as if never extant. Its legacy was me standing there, a relic staring out from a dark, isolated cabin amid thick woods on a secluded lake isle.

I should get to a bedroom, I once again realized, and since standing this time I acted on the thought. I carefully mounted the stairs without benefit of light and was about to turn toward the smaller rooms at back but stopped suddenly in mid-step. My eyes had adjusted to the darkness, could therefore discern the lightest objects, enabling me to perceive a still figure in long white gown standing before the door of the locked room at the front. The face was indistinct but was topped by the whitish coiffure of an elderly woman. We briefly exchanged stares, then she silently turned and retreated to the forbidden room, its lock engaging with a faint click. I continued on to the rearmost room, locked myself in, and lay down to pass the few hours till dawn.

I awoke to the calls of many birds outside the windows, felt grateful for the renewed sunlight, confused about the past night but wanting to forget it awhile. I had my original purpose to pursue, the visit to my relatives. Laura might be worried about my delay. I accordingly got my things together and tried to fashion a breakfast from the staples in the kitchen. I had to settle for oatmeal and, there being no coffee, the strongest among the teas. While preparing my beverage, I saw an empty chamomile packet on the counter that had not been there the day before. My apparition, I mused, but then seriously wondered about her. She did not again appear by the time I left and there was no audible sound from the locked room. Once outside, I noticed that one of the room's windows commanded a clear view of the opening to the access trail.

I did no stumbling about this time as I hiked down to the river. It was a clear, crisp morning that seemed to sweep clear my confusion of the day and night before. Reaching the water's edge, I saw that my borrowed dinghy had been joined by a well-fashioned canoe, much better wrought than those lying in the weeds. Its paddler, small in stature with long dark hair tied back, was examining or sorting some items in a backpack and shopping bags. She smiled as I approached.

"Was everything okay?"

"Yes. But how did you know I was here?"

"He called me." A head tilt toward the mainland. "I came to restock."

"I didn't use much. Not a fan of canned green beans."

She gave a light, tinkling laugh. Just a teenager, I could see. There were cleaning supplies among the items she'd been sorting.

"There is one thing, though. I thought I noticed someone else in there. During the night. As if I wasn't alone."

"Someone else?"

"Yes, a woman. Old like me, maybe even older."

The girl nodded and looked toward the trail, reflecting it seemed. Considering.

"There maybe was someone. I've sensed a presence before when I was here."

She wouldn't lie, I thought, but she could be vague.

"Any idea who she is?"

"There was once another woman there, the teacher's mother, but she has a grave in the town. No one else came to stay. Only renters like yourself."

She moved to pick up her pack and bags preparatory to hiking the trail. The mention of death, as it often does, had clouded our conversation. We wished each other well and she left, I turning to the beached dinghy and another rowing effort. The sun shone brightly off the water.

―――※―――

I'd have liked to question the proprietor further about the teacher's mother, given my experience of the night, but his earlier reluctance to discuss her inhibited me. I therefore simply asked where she'd come from in seeking to escape society, a notion he'd already mentioned.

"Why, the city of course," he answered. "Our state capital. All the hubbub and such, people not giving a damn."

"Think she was happy here?"

"Much as she'd be anywhere else. She had the daughter, a pride and joy. Beyond that I don't know. Like I said before, it was just business between us. Strictly business."

There was a flicker of irritation in his otherwise folksy manner.

I had to let it go. I hadn't mentioned my discovery or hallucination of some hours before.

Back on the road, I felt more than usually grateful for the sunlight and a clear route to my destination. At a growing distance now from the lake isle, I was better able to reflect on the incident there, my face-to-face encounter with a totally unexpected and unknown entity. What was the expression it had? If I'd only been able to discern its face, or if I could enhance the inadequate image in my memory, it might bring precious understanding. The woman, if such she was, had no doubt seen me better, I thought, and it was she who'd first responded by slipping away, but gently, as delicately as possible. Was there meaning in that, a clue to something filed deeply in my psyche? Or were these just random thoughts like in a dream?

I reached the major crossroad in Dooleyville, just as the proprietor had advised, and took it northward to return to my planned route. I reached my destination in the early afternoon, driving through a neat, modern community that indeed looked better for child-rearing than the old neighborhood. The house was a sprawling ranch type in excellent condition.

"Magdalene's having her nap," Laura explained in their living room. "Sammy should be back shortly. Sorry if we gave bad directions."

"No, it was my fault. I should have turned back from the bad turn."

"I hope it wasn't too awful where you stayed overnight."

"Not so awful, no. Kind of interesting, actually."

"Oh?"

She waited expectantly. I told her about Lake of Fire, the proprietor's warning and offer, my night on the lake isle, the spectral figure in the night. I added the scant details I'd heard on the teacher and her officially deceased mother. Laura's expression as I finished became one of grave concern.

"Is something wrong?" I asked.

"No, but--" Laura began. "Did the woman--the figure--you saw by the stairs seem to know you? Did she recognize you? How did she react to you?"

"Well, I couldn't see her face. I only saw her move away. Silently. Go into the room and close the door. What is it, Laura? What are you thinking?"

She hesitated, looking away and inwardly calming herself.

"We never really discussed your mother, you and I."

"No," I acknowledged, "we didn't."

"I suppose it never fit into things. We wanted to get along, needed to."

"And we did and much more. I cherish you, Laura."

She smiled and turned back to me.

"But--" she began, a moment passing. "There was your mother's sudden departure, her return to her clan. There was your father's insecurity all those years, she never making contact."

"Yes," I acknowledged. "She was off at the farm, far away from us. Her family of course took her side, so to speak, were protective of her."

"Did you yourself ever contact them? Or her?"

"No. She was shut away from me, essentially."

"There at the farm. A permanent resident?"

"As far as I knew. The last I ever heard."

Laura sighed heavily.

"Well, some years after your mother left, your father needed to contact her about some real estate legality. His lawyer contacted her family but was told she'd left them and gone to the capital with a hippie by whom she'd borne a child, a little girl."

My interest suddenly peaked. It seemed I had an actual half-sister, a blood relation.

"Did the lawyer track them down?"

"He tried to and partly succeeded. He found the supposed hippie, actually a talented artist who had his own studio and gallery. The artist was quite open about things and said your mother had left him because she couldn't stand the city, the many people and all the activity. She had to get back to a quiet, simple life where she

126

wouldn't feel oppressed by society. She took their daughter with her."

"Did he say where they'd gone?"

"He claimed he didn't know. He said he'd gotten a few notes from her, postmarked in various towns, but none had come for a long time. The last one had come from a place called Dooleyville. The lawyer searched there but came up with nothing. He wasn't too surprised though, going by the last thing your mother said to the artist."

"What was that?"

"She said that she had to find an island somewhere."

I looked at her but did not speak, nothing coming to my mind to say. We sat for a minute or so in silence, in wonderment, amazed by how remote coincidence could upend our settled lives. But maybe just if we let it, I thought.

"I don't suppose Sammy needs to know about this," I said.

"No," Laura agreed, "no need for that at all."

"We'll consider it a dream, imagination in the night."

"While resting from your driving, getting lost."

"Not worth mentioning again."

"No, maybe not ever."

"Never at all."

She went to check on Magdalene and I was alone for a while in the living room. Sammy soon arrived and fixed us all drinks. It was early in the day for me but I felt grateful to him. It helped me to relax amid the sights and sounds of blessed domesticity.

HUMMINGBIRDS IN WINTER

The Castleton case was a special one, and one Victor should not have kept. When he'd described it to his wife Jackie the previous evening, she'd realized that the child's father was someone from her past, an old boyfriend. He was not the suspected abuser--that being a step-father now in the home--but Jackie thought the child could have been hers and felt protective toward him. Vic saw he was in conflict of interest and said he'd get the case transferred to another investigator. But Jackie objected, strongly.

"I want you to keep it," she'd said.

"Why?" he'd asked her.

"I want only you to handle it, not the others. They're strangers to it. They don't know how I care about what happens."

He studied her fervent expression beneath the long brown hair tied back.

"But that's the reason I have to give it up. The personal connection is a conflict of interest."

"Conflict of interest! Like we're in court or something. You can't just slap a label on my feelings, reject them with a rubber stamp!"

Vic hesitated, a bit stunned by her vehemence.

"What do you think I can do that the others cannot?"

"You can do it for me. You can make that special effort that goes beyond professionalism. I trust you with little Byron, more than I trust the others. For them it's another case, but for you it's part of me. I know you'll give it the time, the energy, that won't let mistakes happen. He can't be hurt again. You're the best bet, Vic, so I want you in control."

They'd been married less than a year after a short engagement. He was still getting to know her, the marriage was fragile. He somehow had to accommodate her. She was a part of him now, a vital part of his new inner peace. He could not return to the chaos of before.

"Let me think about it," he said, hoping she herself would and relent.

But then at bedtime it came up again. She stood before him, hair untied, slid the straps of her nightgown over her shoulders. It fell to her feet and covered them like a cloud, she the apparition above.

"This is me asking, Vic, your woman. Do it for me and I'll be happy, complete, a better woman for you. And I'll always be yours. I'll always love you. Please say you'll do it."

On visiting the hospital, Vic was met by a social worker, Linda Century. She was young and small with long red hair, and she wore a smock like a doctor's. She led Vic to her office, small but with a large desk and many plants.

"They're from patients," she explained. "Most of the kids aren't plant lovers but people send them anyway. Some of the kids give them to me. Others were left when a child, well, didn't make it."

Vic noticed some children's photos on the desk.

"Your own?" he asked.

"My nephew and nieces. I see them quite a lot. Between them and the hospital, my life is full of children. I don't know what I'd do if I ever had my own."

Vic brought out his papers.

"Did you get a notice from the court?" he asked.

"They called. I can go myself, but I don't know about Dr. Yee. The doctors are on such tight schedules, they don't like to go unless they're going to testify."

"I'd like for him to be there. He won't for sure have to testify, but it's crucial that we get custody. If we run into any difficulty, the doctor could save the day with his testimony."

"All right. I'll talk to Dr. Yee."

"Good."

"Actually," Linda continued, "he's been very concerned about Byron. We all have. The thought of him going home with that man there, Perkins--well, it's bothered us quite a lot."

"You talked with Perkins?"

"Yes. Well, I tried to. He's not an easy person to talk with. Very insistent, emphatic, on questionable points in his story. He gets worked up emotionally with aggressive body language, calling people offensive names and such."

"Who was he referring to?"

"Once to Dr. Yee, and a couple of times to the man from your agency--Justin, I think his name was."

"Justin Wells, one of our crisis workers."

"Yes. Nobody was pushing Mr. Perkins, accusing him. But I suppose that, when we all kept asking him questions, he concluded we didn't believe him and got defensive, striking out at people. The mother, Melody, is no help with him. Quite passive, defers to him entirely."

"How is Byron feeling now?" Vic asked.

"Much better. The pain has abated so he's getting a milder drug now. He's sleeping well, I've been told. You can see him while you're here, if you like."

"Yes, I'd like to. I'd also like to see the injuries, if that's possible."

"I'll talk to the supervising nurse. Maybe we can get an extra change of dressings."

She looked up at the clock.

"We might as well do it now. The children are in a free period. Later on, they have tests and treatments scheduled."

They left the cubicle and he followed her through the hospital. His briefcase was left with the plants. In relating to Byron, he wanted to be as unimposing as possible, and a briefcase could intimidate. It could cut the boy off from him, costing him a first-hand account of the injuries.

"By the way," Linda said, "Perkins called me just yesterday. He said he wanted our 'conclusions' on the injuries. I told him that any conclusions would be made by DCPS. Then he complained about our making the report. The name-calling bit again."

"Don't worry about him," said Vic. "I'll be talking to him later in the week. He should realize, after the hearing, that his angry routine isn't getting him anywhere."

"I sure hope so."

They came to a nursing station and Linda talked with a nurse about changing the dressings. Vic looked about, eager to locate Byron, but the only children he saw were in a game room at the end of the hall. There were, however, a number of televisions being watched. A cacophony from children's shows filled the corridor.

"She'll send someone later," Linda reported.

They proceeded to one of the rooms. On the bed nearest the door, a heavy boy of seven or eight was lounging in his robe, watching the destruction of an advanced civilization on TV. On the bed by the window lay a smaller boy, dark-haired and somber, flipping the pages of a colorful book. His feet and ankles were bandaged.

"George," Linda addressed the heavy boy, "this man has to talk to Byron. Can you watch TV in the clubhouse?"

"That show is dumb," came the reply.

But he agreed when promised an extra jello at lunchtime. The invading space-squads were abruptly shut off, the focus of attention becoming the boy by the window. He paid no heed to the quieting of the television or the departure of his roommate. But when he saw the adults coming, Linda and the stranger, he stopped flipping pages and watched them. He especially studied Vic, who looked back into clear, greenish eyes. The investigator smiled as Byron continued to gaze. The smile was not returned, however.

"Byron," said Linda, "this is Mr. Walton. He came here to visit you. You can talk to him about anything you want."

"Are you a doctor?" asked the boy.

"No," Vic replied.

"A policeman?"

"No."

"A garbage man?"

"No."

"What are you, then? Are you from outer space?"

"No, I'm not. I'm from an office, a place where they send out guys to be friends with boys in hospitals."

Byron was silent a moment. Then he turned to Linda.

"How come they sent a guy to me but not to George?"

"Well, I don't know. Maybe Mr. Walton can be George's friend, too."

"Call me Vic," said the visitor.

He waited for Byron to talk again, hoping for a lead he could follow in asking his questions.

"Are you going to eat here?" asked the boy. "The pudding is good but the oatmeal is yuck!"

"I can't do it today," Vic answered, "but maybe next time. Tell you what. Next time I come, I'll bring you something really good to eat. Would you like that?"

"Yes," said Byron, but still without a smile. "How come you can't eat here today?"

"I'm having lunch with another guy who visits boys in hospitals. His name is Bernie."

"Bring Bernie here so he can visit George!"

"Oh, well, that's an idea. Tell you what. I'll ask him about it."

"Byron," Linda spoke up, "why don't you tell Vic about your feet?"

Vic was taken aback. He hoped that what she said had not been too direct.

"I hurt my feet," said Byron.

"Oh," Vic responded. "That's too bad. Are they getting better?"

"Yes. I don't have to take the pills like footballs any more. Now I take pills like baseballs."

"Oh. Well, that's much better. Tell me, Byron, when was it you hurt your feet? Do you remember what day it was?"

"It was Saturday."

"Saturday?"

"Yes, but maybe Sunday. It was a day my mama goes out."

"She goes out Saturday and Sunday?"

"Yes, to find the hummingbirds."

"Hummingbirds?"

"Yes, to find where they are in winter. She hasn't found them yet. Do you know where they go in the winter?"

"Well, I--" Vic faltered. "I guess I don't know."

He didn't like to directly question a child about his abuse. He stayed on the periphery, helping the child recall the circumstances. Eventually, he thought, the child would describe the incident on his own. The information he volunteered, Vic reasoned, would be more accurate than that given to satisfy an adult. It was important to utilize the childhood capacity for frankness. The younger the child, the greater this capacity--as long as he could talk. At age five, Byron seemed an ideal witness to the cause of his injuries.

"Byron," Vic continued, "do you remember where you were when you got hurt?"

"I was at my house, the apartment."

He had some difficulty with the final word. But, Vic reflected, it was a long word for such a small boy.

"Can you remember what room you were in?"

Byron turned suddenly to Linda.

"Is it time for lunch yet?"

"No. Not yet, Byron. We still have time to talk with Mr. Walton."

"How long are you staying?" Byron asked Vic. "Are you going to go pretty soon?"

"Yes, Byron, I am. But first I want to see them change your bandages. The nurse will be coming to do it soon."

"How come you have to watch?"

"I want to make sure they're doing it right."

"Why?"

"Because I'm your friend."

That seemed to satisfy the boy. He was calm. Vic decided to give it another shot.

"Byron, on the day you got hurt, was there anybody else in the apartment? Or were you by yourself?"

"I can't stay by myself. I'm not old enough."

"So, somebody else was there?"

Byron was silent.

"Do you think maybe your grandma was there? How about George? Was he there?"

"No. George wasn't there."

"Well, how about your grandma? Was she there when you got hurt?"

"Gramma doesn't go there. We just go to her house. She makes macaroni in a big brown pot. Do you like macaroni?"

"Uh, yes. I love it. But say, Byron, if your grandma wasn't there, and George wasn't there, do you remember--can you give me the name of someone who was in the apartment when you got hurt?"

Byron shifted about, restless. Linda took his hand.

"Do you remember who was there?" she asked.

"Some people were there," he said.

"Can you tell Vic their names?"

"No. I don't know who they were. I can't remember. Maybe it was a dream. Can you get burned in a dream?"

The social worker hesitated.

"I don't know," she said softly.

A young nurse came in and proceeded to change the dressings. Vic braced himself as she cut off the first bandage, then viewed the mending flesh with forced calm. He wasn't supposed to be angry. It was all right for the police, for anyone else involved. But it wasn't all right for child abuse investigators. They were expected to be objective in their assessments. Their sympathies belonged with the total family unit, including the abuser, and personal outrage could not be allowed to color their findings. Nonetheless, Vic was angry. He often was, and so were the other investigators. And this time, as he recalled Jackie's statements, he was especially angry. He felt a deep, cold antipathy toward the creature that had burned Byron.

The burns extended from the tip of each foot to a point about two inches above each ankle, at which point there was a sharp lateral division between seared and unharmed flesh. This was consistent with the report. As Vic looked closely, however, it appeared that the right foot might be burned slightly more than the left, the burn line extending about half an inch higher and the color of the burn a bit deeper. He envisioned Byron being placed in the water. Perhaps he'd gone in at an angle, so that the right foot entered first and he had to stand on it as he withdrew his left. But Vic wouldn't dwell on the point. He might just be grabbing at a technicality to escape the terror of the total incident. And he couldn't afford to escape. Byron had already done that. Vic had to probe the reality, ugly as it was, and publicly clarify what Byron couldn't. He had to protect a little boy who could not protect himself.

"The water must have been awful hot," said Vic. "It's surprising it could do that coming from the tap."

They were returning to Linda's office.

"Maybe he warmed the tub first," she said. "He could have run some hot water, let it out, then filled the tub so it'd be hotter. He could have boiled some, too. Or maybe they're right by the boiler room. Did you notice on your visit?"

"No. They're at ground level, but I didn't check the adjacent units. I'll be going there Friday. I can check it then."

They came to the room with the plants and Vic retrieved his briefcase.

"Actually," said the social worker, "Byron is almost ready for discharge as far as the burns go. They can be treated in the home with an ointment. However, I've asked for a psychological assessment. We'll be staffing the case next week, after he's seen by the psychiatrist and psychologist. We have to decide about follow-up treatment for the blockage Byron is showing."

"Right," said Vic. "I'd like to know what you decide on that. And I guess you'll let me know if Byron says anything about the abuse."

"I will."

"Thanks. And if Perkins calls again, you can refer him to me."

She looked relieved. Though she knew her job and worked at it hard, she had her limits. Vic felt good when he helped her with them. It was a professional exchange, each of them helping the other and together helping Byron, whose welfare was the focus of their agencies. It filled Vic with a sense of social worth, a quiet pride that he hadn't known inspecting auto damage, his last job. And yet, on leaving the room with many plants, Ms. Century at her at her big metal desk, Vic realized that he hadn't accomplished much. With Byron's refusal to talk, in fact, he'd acquired a new problem. He now had to labor to support his case without the testimony or support of either the boy or Melody, his mother. Perkins, meanwhile, could claim to be a first-hand witness with the support, presumably, of his children. Or could the support of Scott and Bree be weakened, even reversed? He'd have to give it a try.

The theater from which Vic had ordered tickets was large but shabby. plywood applied over missing glass. A poster stapled to the plywood advertised the play, *Ghost of Orgasm*. It pictured a wispy apparition hovering over a man and woman in bed. The man was noticeably older. Vic was ready to turn and leave but then remembered his promise to Jackie. He shouldn't provide a subject for disagreement. Not now, when he had so much to do. So he went in and picked up the tickets. He reflected that, ordinarily, he wouldn't have cared how silly the play was. It would be enough for him that she wanted to see it. Now, however, with the pressures of Castleton in their life, to be occupied with something trivial seemed wrong, a mistake that disrupted the focus of his energies on a vital project. But then Jackie, obviously, didn't see it that way. He had no choice but to see the play with her, to shove his resentment to a far corner of his mind.

Instead of driving to the office, Vic stopped at Peppercorn's, a beer-and-chili joint that he and Bernie had adopted as a weekly adventure. His coworker was already in a booth, munching on tiny crackers and knocking the crumbs from his beard. Vic approached over a creaky wooden floor.

"How's the chili today?" he asked. "You get enough kidney beans?"

"Yes," Bernie replied. "Big ones, too. Maybe they're real kidneys."

A middle-aged waitress took Vic's order. Bernie kept spooning his chili, looking humble in his herringbone jacket with patched elbows. Vic liked that about him. While Bernie was sensitive and capable of strong assertions, he offered himself as a calm, unaggressive sort who was ready to absorb your problems. Vic felt the urge to unload some Castleton on him. But that wouldn't be right just now. They came here to get away, to have a little relief from the pressures of the job. He should talk about something else.

"How's your heat now?" he asked.

"Better," said Bernie, "but not good enough. It was 59 degrees when I got up this morning. I had to call him again."

"Does he know what's wrong?"

"He says it's set right, but it keeps shutting off too soon."

"Think he's leveling with you?"

"Who knows? Anyway, it's not my problem now. I left it up to him. Either he gets it fixed or I call the mayor's office."

"I guess that should do it, then."

"He got the message."

Chili and crackers were laid before Vic. Taking a swig of beer, he reflected that some tenseness Bernie had shown the prior day was gone. He was more open, accessible. Maybe, Vic thought, he could talk a bit about Jackie. He wanted to share, somehow, the bulky load of problems that were weighing on him. And Bernie, after all, should understand. He too was married without children, and they performed the same job.

"So, how's Eva?" Vic asked.

Bernie's spoon stopped halfway to his mouth, his eyebrows rising. In a moment, however, he was the same as before.

"She's fine," he said. "Fine."

But then came the familiar frown beneath the black curls and Bernie laid down his spoon.

"She wants me to quit," he said.

Vic looked at him without responding. The subject of Jackie dispersed like a mist.

"She wants me to take a job with her uncle. He has a business on the North Side, retirement hotels."

"Has he made you an offer?"

"A standing offer, I guess. I didn't think he was serious, but Eva says he is. I mean, I see him at family gatherings. He has a few drinks and starts talking. I never thought he meant it. Now, I guess she's been talking with her parents and the offer's for real. They mentioned a specific opening."

Bernie signaled for another beer.

"So," said Vic, "how do you feel about it?"

"I don't know. I'm doing all right here, I think. We have our share of hassles, of course, our share of ugliness--some really bad times. But who knows what the new job would be like? I might well regret the move. Plus, I'd have to face her relatives if I wanted out."

"What kind of job is it?"

"Managing one of his older buildings. I'm supposed to get all the details when I go for the interview."

"Are you going?"

"I don't know. I don't want to, but I have to think things out. My wife, you see--"

His voice broke off as he gestured in the air. Then the gesture collapsed as well. He brightened a bit as a full stein was set before him.

"I'll have another, too," Vic told the waitress.

"It's not just the offer from Uncle Mike," said Bernie. "Even without his offer, Eva doesn't like my working at DCPS."

"Why's that?"

"She doesn't like to hear about it at home. Says I sound morbid. She also thinks it affects my personality--makes me dark, brooding.

It turns her off. She wants me to be in something more businessy. So we can laugh and joke more about our jobs. Upbeat. She wants to be upbeat."

Vic studied the subsiding foam in his beer.

"Funny thing," he said. "Jackie doesn't feel that way. She's always been interested in my work, especially lately. Of course, Eva's a teacher, with bright, happy children all day, while Jackie's selling old collectibles. I guess she's a little hungrier to discuss people, even abused children. I sometimes wish, though, that she'd take a little less of an interest."

"Why?"

The answer was a single word: Castleton. But Vic had to say something else.

"So our relationship could develop along other lines."

Bernie looked puzzled.

"But our careers are so central to our lives. How can they not be central to a relationship? And why shouldn't they be?"

"Well," Vic answered, "I'm not saying it's bad. And for sure it's good to some extent. Obviously, it's important to you and Eva. It's important to us, too. But I guess I was thinking of something more basic, something that takes up where our jobs leave off."

He hesitated. Bernie was listening with eyebrows up, his intensity giving way to calm sophistication.

"I was thinking," Vic said, "of a partnership of spirits, rather than mentalities. Where, more and more, the man and woman realize the best values to have, the best way to live. Where a kind of magnetism sets in from the knowledge that they practice, together, the highest level of human experience."

Bernie smiled a bit.

"Does this involve religion?"

"No, it involves--"

Vic looked away, searching for words.

"It involves a special and unique refinement that makes us, as human beings, like gods to each other!"

Bernie's smile widened and Vic knew what was coming. The

beard tilted upward and a familiar horselaugh rocked the booth. People looked over, forgetting their bowls and steins. Bernie's eyes were tear-filled as the laugh subsided, his face flush with merriment.

"Vic," he said, "you must have had a couple before you came."

Vic smiled, surrendering to hilarity. He had meant what he said, but he saw how it could sound funny. It wasn't just the words he'd used. It was more the attempt to be honest without revealing the secret of Castleton. Jackie's involvement in the case gave it overriding importance that chained him to his profession, and to the dark lives of the people he investigated. It put him off the course that he and Jackie had been taking to sublime, intelligent joy, grounded in confidence.

Bernie, Vic decided, should not have laughed so loud.

———

It was the laugh that did it, Vic decided later--cleared the fog from his thinking and set him on his closing course. He spent all afternoon in the office, writing up his morning's activity and a summary of his work on Castleton. The summary would be needed because of a memo he'd be leaving his supervisor. It told of Jackie's connection to the case, and of his perception it should be reassigned. In it he apologized for the delay in reporting, as well as his continued involvement with the case, and he offered to resign. He left the memo in a sealed envelope on his supervisor's desk after the office had closed.

It might be the end with Jackie, too, Vic thought as he walked to his car. But as she herself had said, Byron deserved the best in protective services. Those could not be given by a compromised investigator.

———

Some weeks after inheriting the Castleton case, Bernie learned that Byron had been placed in the tub by Scott and Bree, Perkins's children. The follow-up therapist for Byron had used small dolls to have him reenact the incident. The children were playing a game inspired by something they'd seen on television, Perkins not present since he was working on his car in the parking lot. Bernie decided to wait for evening to inform Victor, not wanting to distract his friend in his claims adjusting. They were both "free men" again, wives having left them due to their job decisions. It was a matter of existential choice, Bernie thought.

The hummingbirds, he'd found out for Byron, did not go anywhere in winter. They stayed around where they always were, but in a state of shock, not quite hibernation, with little activity so they didn't need much food. They withdrew from the world awhile in order to survive.

www.ingramcontent.com/pod-product-compliance
Lightning Source LLC
Chambersburg PA
CBHW030519260626
47157CB00005B/1809